Taking Chances

Passion Series Books 1 and 2

Hope Wilkie-Summers

DEDICATION

In memory of Violet Cadle

12th November 1939- 28th October 2023

I miss you so much Nan, more than you know, and I hope you're watching me from Heaven. Enjoy the company of Tiggy and the jokes from Matthew Perry. I love you to the moon and back.

Also by Hope Wilkie-Summers

Standalone

Up In Flames

A Murder In The Mansion

How Do You Love Someone

Taking Chances

ACKNOWLEDGMENTS

I'd like to thank everyone who has made this one possible. Writing my first book has been such a fun journey and I'm so thankful to have had the support from my family.
Nan, you were always boosting me up when I needed you and I know you're still doing that from above the clouds. I only became an author because you wanted to read the stories I was always writing.
Thank you to my book group too. George, Emma, Chelsie, thanks for keeping me smiling every day.

UP IN FLAMES

CHAPTER 1

I re-read the email on my laptop several times. I'd
done it. I'd got the job as stage assistant for the local
theatre's production of Cinderella. It looked easy. The
interview was fun and it got me really excited, I
started the next morning.
"Addison!" Mum called upstairs. "Come downstairs
for dinner please!"
"Coming!" I called back as I logged off my laptop.
It was just mum and me at home; my Dad had left us
when I was a few years old for someone from his
office at work. They were married now. I was
eighteen and fresh out of college now so that was
long in the past for me.
"I got the job at the theatre." I told her as we sat
down in the living room, our plates on trays on our
laps. "Well done sweetie. Are you sure you want a job
this quickly? I mean, you only finished college last
month." Concern wrinkled her face.
"Yes, we need the money." That was all that I replied
with.

"Addy, you're eighteen! Worrying about money is my responsibility, you need to enjoy life and leave it to me."

Ever since Dad left, I'd begun to notice mum was struggling. Open bills left on the kitchen counter, letters about bank loans opened on her bedside table. It had started to worry me so all I'd wanted was to help mum like she'd helped me my whole life. She didn't want to accept my help, obsessed with putting on a brave face for me. I still saw her struggling.

The next morning, I woke up full of excitement. It was my first day working at the theatre. I wasn't going to wear anything formal, so I chose my black skinny jeans and a pink top.

Mum had already left for work by the time I went to the kitchen to get breakfast. I quickly made myself some toast before grabbing my bag and heading out the door. I locked it before putting the keys safely in my pocket.

The sun was shining and the sky a pale, cloudless blue as I walked to the bus stop. A gentle breeze drifted through my hair. People walked their dogs in the park over the bush to my left, all I could hear was barking. I arrived just in time to get the bus, it pulled into the bus stop as I got there. It was a twenty minute bus ride.

I loved the theatre. It was situated in the town's high street and was next to Poundland and opposite the library. It was huge, taking up a third of the left side of the high street. It had two sets of double doors and a huge poster advertising Cinderella outside of it.

First day. To say the truth, I was really nervous. Plucking up the courage, I stepped through one of the sets of double doors. As I walked through the chandelier lit lobby, I made a mental note to not let anything distract me from this job. What I didn't know was that that was about to go straight out the window.

Everyone was waiting for me when I got to the huge auditorium.

"Sorry I'm late." I called out as I took my seat with the stage manager and director. I knew them both from my interview. Their names were Freddy and Tyler.

"You're not late Addison." said Tyler, the director. "In fact, now we're just waiting on our lead actor." The doors opened as he said that and the actor for Prince Charming came in.

My heart skipped a beat and my breath got caught in my throat.

My eyes widened as I took in every detail of him. Black hair, piercing blue eyes, high cheekbones and a smile that could easily melt hearts. It definitely melted mine. He wore jeans and a red t-shirt. I sucked in a breath as he sat in the seat opposite mine. I shifted my attention back to the director.

"Now that Jake's arrived," Tyler said as he looked at Jake "We can begin rehearsals." Lucky for me, the cast had already been decided four weeks ago so people should know most of their lines. Today we were going to begin memorising lines for each scene. As the actors walked up the steps to the stage, Freddy came over with a basket full of folders.

"These are for you Addy. It's everyone's contact information, all of the casting and everything you need to know as stage assistant." He handed me the basket. Oh my gosh, why were they so heavy? Surely I didn't need all of this. Worst part was that I had to

3

take most of them to and from the theatre every day. I spent the session reading through the folders. I paid the most attention to the script and everyone's contact details in case of an emergency. At that point, being a stage assistant didn't feel as important as I'd thought it would be.

I looked briefly to Jake, stood in the center of the stage, before looking away. Alarm bells rang strongly in my mind. Why did Jake seem like a huge distraction? I looked up again for a second and gasped as his eyes locked on mine. I cleared my throat.

The day passed pretty quickly and before I knew it, we were done for the day. I avoided all types of contact with anyone; I needed to stay focused. I kept my head down as I left the theatre. It was a pain carrying all of those folders home. It was starting to drizzle as I walked to the bus stop. Too bad for me that I'd forgotten a coat. I stood under a tree so that I was as sheltered from the rain as possible. The folders were beginning to get soaked so I pulled them closer into me. I stumbled under their weight as I got on the bus.

Mum was getting ready to go out as I got in.

"Where are you going?" I asked as I put the heavy folders on the kitchen counter.

"Not far, just a few drinks with a few friends." She said, slipping on her black flats. "I've left you something in the microwave if you don't feel like cooking for yourself."

"Thanks mum." She kissed my head as she left. I hadn't realised it was almost seven already.

I spent the rest of the evening reading through everyone's contact details. After about half an hour, my phone started ringing. No caller ID. I accepted the call.

"Hello?" I asked uncertainly.

"Addison? It's Tyler." I breathed a sigh of relief.

"Hi Tyler, what's up?"

"I just called to tell you something that I forgot to mention at the theatre."

"I didn't do anything wrong did I?" Panic coated my tone.

"No no no. I forgot to tell you that you'll be working in close contact with Jake. Freddy has a lot to do already as stage manager already, so he'll need you with Jake making sure he gets everything right and remembers his lines."

That wasn't what I was expecting him to say. Working in close contact with Jake every day? I needed to get my emotions in check as quickly as possible.

"Everything okay Addison?" Tyler asked, his voice sounding concerned.

"Yes, everything's fine. I'm just reading all of the information that Freddy gave me earlier." And completely freaking out.

"Oh ok. We've informed Jake that he'll be with you a lot and he sounded really excited about it."

"Oh did he now?" I hadn't thought he'd even noticed me except for that moment when our eyes locked. Apart from that, he'd looked at everyone else except for me. Not that I cared.

"Yes. Anyway, I'll let you go so that you're ready for another long day of work tomorrow." Tyler hung up before I had a chance to say anything more.

It took me a while to get to sleep that night. I was still trying to absorb everything that had happened today. I heard mum get home around ten and I fell asleep not long after.

Next morning I was ready to go. I was looking forward to today's rehearsals. I had a quick shower and a bowl of cereal. I wrote a note for mum on the kitchen counter saying I was leaving early and that I'd see her later.

Full of confidence, I threw open the theatre door and hit something on the other side.

"Ow!" Someone yelped.

"I'm so sorry! I didn't expect anyone to be stood there, are you okay?" I said as I dashed to see if they were okay. Jake smiled at me. Those eyes could make you melt I swear.

"Yeah, I'm fine, no hard feelings. I'm guessing that you're Addison?" I nodded. "Cool, I'm looking forward to spending a lot of time together."

My heart skipped a beat. Tyler was right.

"Shall we go somewhere quiet and look over the script?" I asked as I walked towards a dressing room that I knew never got used.

"Sure." Jake followed me in and closed the door behind us.

CHAPTER 2

I underestimated the size of this dressing room. It
was a tiny box of a room with two chairs in a corner
and a mirror hung on the opposite wall. Jake and I
were sat so close together that I could smell the mint
toothpaste he'd used that morning. I was surprised at
how well he seemed to know the script. Had he been
up all night learning the script like I'd been trying to?
Jake cleared his throat. "So, will you tell me a bit
about yourself Addison?"

"You can call me Addy." A blush rose up in my
cheeks. "There's not really much to know. Is there
anything specific you'd like the answer to?" I didn't
know what else to say. I silently prayed he wasn't
flirting or trying to distract me from my job.

We spent the next hour asking questions about each
other. I learned quite a lot about his childhood and
what he enjoyed doing as he grew up. He was an
outdoor person; he loved the beach and climbing
trees with his friends

After what was probably two hours, Tyler burst into

the dressing room.

"Addison, I have a dilemma!" he cried, flustered. His face was white, the look of stress.

"Whatever's the matter?" I asked.

"I need you to be the understudy for Cinderella. We can't find anyone who we think will suit the role, let alone learn all the lines with miraculous speed. As stage assistant, you need good knowledge of everyone's lines anyway. So what do you say?"

My breath got caught in my throat. Me? Act? As the understudy for a lead role? It wasn't exactly what I'd applied for … Although I'd only go on stage if something happened to the original actress.

"Perfect! You've saved me more stress than I'm already dealing with. Have fun working on the script." I swear I saw Tyler wink at me before his eyes flickered to Jake as he left.

I couldn't believe I'd just agreed to the possibility of acting onstage. What on earth was I thinking? The last time I performed onstage was three years ago. It was my Year 11 leaver's ceremony from secondary school. It wasn't the main role, but I was pretty close. As soon as I stepped onto the stage to deliver my scene, I broke down with a huge panic attack. I thought I'd let the team down.

I desperately wanted to have a career in theatre, so I got myself involved in everything. I studied drama at college and was constantly surfing the internet for anything; pantomimes, plays, productions… Literally anything that involved theatre. Then I saw the advert for Cinderella and applied for every backstage role that was still available. Et voila! Now I was the stage assistant and Cinderella's understudy. I just hoped I was over my stage fright by now.

"So you're an actress now too?" Jake joked as I snapped out of my reverie.

"It would appear so. To be honest, I can't really believe that I agreed to it." I explained to him the story of my stage fright.

"You'll be fine Addy, I promise." He smiled and leant in a little closer to me. Our noses were almost touching.

"I hope so."

That evening, I spent the whole time reading Cinderella's parts over and over again. Over dinner, I told mum the news about my understudy role.

"You'll do great. Keep your focus and you'll do absolutely perfect." Were her words of wisdom.

So I'd been up in my room memorising the script ever since. I was getting really good at the first scene. I'd lost track of the time by the time I finally fell asleep.

I woke up the next morning feeling grateful that it was Saturday. I'd been up into the early hours of the morning working on that damned script. I was glad to have a day to myself; no Jake to distract me. I could get everything done that I needed to, assuming mum didn't make me run any errands for her.

After I'd got up and showered, I decided to cook mum and I fried egg and bacon rolls for breakfast. I'd always loved the sound of bacon as it sizzled in the pan. Once it was cooked, I called mum and she came and sat at the kitchen table.

"I'm going out for a couple hours if that's ok sweetie."

I nodded. "Of course it is. I've got a few things I need to get done anyway."

We said our goodbyes and I went upstairs to my

room.

I sat on my bedroom floor with the script out in front of me. My highlighter was on stand-by for when Cinderella came up.

I still couldn't believe that I'd agreed to it. Although I couldn't back out now, I had to get on with it. I spent half of the day memorising and the other half doing housework whilst mum was out. I cleaned the kitchen and did some gardening. Gardening in my words is usually just weeding. I'm not exactly known to have green thumbs. After I'd cooked dinner for myself, mum was still out, I laid on the sofa and began reading my book.

Something was shaking me. I opened my eyes.

"Addy, it's after eight. How long have you been there?" Mum laughed softly.

"I laid down to read my book after having my dinner around four. I must have fallen asleep."

"Go on up to bed. That theatre is keeping you busy, isn't it?"

Mum and I both walked up the stairs, brushed our teeth and then went our separate ways to our bedroom for the night.

The next morning, mum came in holding a stack of pancakes under my nose. They were dripping with maple syrup and had an assortment of blueberries, raspberries and strawberries on top. They smelled so fresh and looked delicious, it was making me salivate.

"Thank you." I smiled gratefully as she handed me the plate along with a knife and fork.

"Enjoy the theatre today sweetie."

I sliced through the pancakes. They were so light and fluffy on my tongue. I ate them quickly then put my plate on my bedside table before heading into the bathroom. I stepped into the shower and felt my muscled relax as the hot water ran all over my body. I kept the temperature as high as it would go, it never burned me. I washed myself with the rose scented shower gel my mum had bought me recently. It was a strong scent but it was perfect for the summer season we were in.

We had 5 months until the show would premiere. 5 months to get everything perfect and all lines remembered. That morning, I swore to myself I wouldn't become distracted by anyone or anything, it was crucial the show went without a hitch. The cast had been selected so there was one less thing to worry about. Our first performance would be in early November and it was just about to become June. Already almost all of the tickets for opening night had been booked.

I stepped out of the shower and wrapped myself in a towel. Within minutes I was dressed and blow drying my hair in front of my bedroom mirror. Perhaps if we all arrived early we'd have longer to work on things, I thought to myself. Everything needed to be perfect. It was raining when I went outside so I was annoyed at the time I'd wasted drying my hair. I put my hood up on my coat to keep as much of it dry as I possibly could. I knew mum still wasn't keen on the idea of me already working to pay bills, she wanted to be independent and not need help. She'd always been that way. Wind blew strongly as I walked to the bus stop. People swayed as they walked from the strength the wind was pushing at us. Birds were staying in the trees, not flying. I kept a fast pace as I walked. The bus was there when I arrived so I joined onto the end of the queue.

"Can I have a return ticket to town please?" I asked the driver. He had a blue jacket with the bus company embroidered into it and a blue hat on his curly brown hair.

"Of course." I put my card under the card machine and waited for it to beep. He printed out my ticket and passed it to me.

"Thank you." I smiled. I walked down the aisle to find a seat towards the back of the bus. I preferred the back seats so I was away from any screaming children. I found a seat and pulled out the script. Why I was now Cinderella's understudy as well as stage assistant was something I'd never know. I hoped I wouldn't need to act, I had terrible stage fright. I had studied drama in secondary school as a GCSE subject and completely hated it. I'd thought it meant we'd be able to perform and do the backstage jobs as well, but my oh my was I wrong. It was all performance which to me didn't make sense because backstage was the most important role. They were the people who kept everything together and running smoothly, it wasn't just down to the actors. Backstage members are the people who keep everything in line and make sure it's all perfect; the set, whether lines had been rehearsed, giving prompts when needing, blocking the scenes. They were the most important roles and I was feeling so lucky to have a chance to show my skills to everyone. I was a small part of a huge team, but I would make a difference. Just as long as I didn't get distracted.

The last time I'd performed onstage was horrible. It had been for my GCSE assessment. I'd been given an onstage role and denied a backstage one no matter how many times I'd explained how uncomfortable I felt onstage. A few other students studying the subject had been invited to watch the performance. I was full of nerves and anxiety from the moment I'd opened my eyes that day. I knew my teacher knew how badly I didn't want to do it.

"You'll be fine Addy." She had said when she saw how pale I'd become. We were due to start in five minutes. "If I didn't think you could do it, I wouldn't have given you this role."

Shortly into the performance was where it all began to go wrong for me. I was sick halfway through. I'd ran off the stage with the understudy following closely behind me. I was amazed at how I'd gotten to the toilets in time before it came up and I collapsed to the floor in a pile of tears. There were so many faces staring at the stage, it was scary. After that, I knew I wanted a career in theatre, just not one where I wanted to be in the spotlight.

As the bus drove, I turned my attention out of the window. I watched the cars blur past and the wind as it swayed the trees. I heard the sound of dogs barking over the rain pounding on the roof. I put the script away into my bag and kept my gaze outside. I loved the heat of summer, just not the rain. Although where I lived the weather did as it pleased, rather than go off the seasons like it should've. That was the one thing I could never stand living here; the weather. People got on and off at every stop. My spirits lifted slightly when I caught a glimpse of the sun trying to break its way through the clouds.

The driver called out my stop and I pressed the button. The bus came to a stop.

"Thank you." I smiled as I got off the bus. The rain had begun to slow, the sun forcing its presence to be known. Birds were starting to come out, I could see a few flying above me.

I arrived at the theatre still soaked. Almost everyone was already there before I'd arrived. Jake smiled up at me as I walked through the doors to the main backstage rehearsal room. I gave him a discreet wave and sat up near Freddy and Tyler.

"I trust lines are almost memorised?" Freddy called out once everyone was here. "Because today I think we'll start to block the first couple of scenes. Addison, you'll be needed today. Especially your opinion on how you think it all looks."

"Ok." I nodded.

"Shall we get started?"

Freddy and Tyler led us all into the main theatre space and we sat in the rows of seats at the front. The lights had been dimmed.

"Vanessa, please go brighten up the lights." Tyler asked.

"Of course." Vanessa got up and walked to the back of the room. She had a small frame and delicate features. Blond hair framed her face and her hazel eyes stood out against the paleness of her skin. She was wearing a floral patterned dress and small white heeled shoes. The lights brightened up a bit and we began working.

Tyler made his way up the steps to the stage and called up Jake and Cinderella, Lauren I think her name was.

"Addison, while you wait for me to need your support, please look over the script at Lauren's lines."

"Of course."

I got up and walked a few rows back so I could get a little bit of peace to allow myself to focus. I was still feeling really unsure about being an understudy. It had been a few years since my exam performance, but I still didn't think I'd have miraculously gained enough confidence not to get sick again.

They were blocking out the first few scenes for quite a while, I kept peering up every now and then. My excitement lay behind set painting, not being upon a stage. After about an hour, I heard my name.

"What do you think?" The director asked me. "From the top!"

I watched as Cinderella and her father were looking after the animals on the farm when she was younger, I saw a little glimpse into the scene where her father dies. The expressions and body language used really set the tone and showed the emotions being portrayed in the scene.

"I like it. It really shows how happy Ella is in her youth with her father. With the set behind it and the lighting sorted, I think scene one will be perfect as it is." I praised while I silently praying I hadn't dug myself a hole.

"Well if you think so, then I'm sure everyone else will." Freddy said.

"I loved it too! I think we've got the first scene down." Vanessa chipped in. I threw a grateful smile her way and she returned it.

By the end of the day, the first two scenes had been blocked. Tomorrow was set for me to start painting the set. No pun intended. We all said our goodbyes and I decided to head up the high street rather than towards home. The wind streaked through my hair and the sun was slightly covered by clouds. The fresh smell of the sea was carried in the wind. I headed up the high street towards the fish and chip shop. Mum would enjoy a treat.

The high street was filled with shut down shops, charity shops and places like Poundland. It wasn't anything like how I remembered it had been when I was younger. Back then every shop was open and busy all through the day. The market thrived when compared to how dead it was now. People preferred to shop online these days because it was convenient for them, but a community needed everyone to play a part. Nobody did anymore because nobody tried. I didn't have any issues with charity shops, but they aren't the best when you wanted to shop somewhere local for birthdays or Christmas. For that, you'd have to travel to the next town before you found anything. I grew excited at the smell of fresh chips being wafted towards me. When I was younger, we'd have fish and chips from the chippy every Friday night as a treat. But they became infrequent when the unopened bills began piling up and up. I'd saved my childhood allowance from mum through my teens and only bought for emergencies, so I thought I'd treat mum to an old tradition. A small taste of nostalgia. It was a small take-away shop; no attached restaurant like some chippies have now. I loved the smell of the chips, the fish, the grease and the sausages as I walked in. I breathed in the comforting smell before ordering.

"Hi, can I have 2 small pieces of cod and 2 large chips please?" I asked the lady at the counter. She had dyed pink hair and bright blue eyes.

"Of course. Any drinks?" She asked.

"No thank you."

She called out the order and I heard the sizzling sound of fish being put into the fryers. She bagged up our chips as the fish was lifted out the fryer and drained of the excess oil.

"Salt and vinegar?" She asked as she picked up the salt shaker.

"Salt on one and both on the other please."

She bagged up the fish, put both bags in a plastic bag and handed it to me.

"Ten pounds please." She asked. I held my bank card out and tapped it on the card machine.

"Thank you." I said again as I left the shop. I made my way to the bus station. I knew the food would most likely be cold once I was home, but it's the thought that counted.

As I'd guessed, it was cold when I got home. Mum was upstairs so I hoped the smell hadn't wafted up to her so it could be a proper surprise. I portioned it onto two plates and gave each a three minute blast in the microwave. I knew mum wouldn't complain, she'd just be happy to have a take-away.

"Mum!" I called. "Come downstairs." I heard a groan from somewhere upstairs then the muffled sound of walking. Mum appeared downstairs just over a minute later.

"Yes?" She asked.

"Dinner."

I felt a giant wave of happiness wash over me as I saw her face light up. Her cheeks lifted and she smiled the biggest smile I'd seen her have in years. I never thought such a little thing could bring someone so much happiness. We sat and ate in the living room. We didn't have a dining room; we'd converted it into a study a few years ago. We watched TV with our plates on our laps, a bottle of ketchup on the floor between us.

"Thanks for this sweetie." Mum said and turned to face me.

"It's ok mum, you deserve a treat. It's been ages since we've had the chippy so I picked it up on the way home for us."

"You're the sweetest girl, you really are. I'm so lucky to have you. I'm so so sorry I haven't been able to give you the life you deserve, the childhood you should have had. I wanted to give you so much but I couldn't, whether that was money or time. I worked every spare minute once your dad left us to try to make ends meet and I struggled a lot. I still struggle, as you know. I'm proud of you for getting yourself a job, but once you told me why you'd applied for it, I knew you'd noticed. I hadn't hid everything as well as I'd thought I had and I'm sorry. I haven't meant to worry you sweetie, it's just taken a while to sort things." Tears pooled in mum's eyes and one slipped onto her cheek when she looked up to me. I threw my arms around her.

"You don't need to be sorry, I've loved every moment with you mum. It's been perfect. I got my job as early as I have because I wanted to help so you won't be as stressed out as you have been. You're my mum and you've looked after me so it's my turn to look after you." She still had tears in her eyes when I pulled away.

CHAPTER 3

It was sunny when I woke up the next morning. I was doing set design today and I could already feel my creative juices flowing.

I still felt sorry for mum after everything she told me yesterday. Even though she was upset I'd got this job to help her, I knew she'd be grateful for it in the long run because it would ease some of the pressure she was under. She needed to know that it was ok to ask me for help. I knew she how much she hated admitting to needing help, but I was her daughter. She wasn't home when I went downstairs for breakfast, I assumed she'd left early for work. Mum worked in the supermarket in the next town over. She'd struggled applying for jobs after being fired for taking time off after my dad left and that was the only place that had accepted her. Whether or not she liked the job, I had no idea, but I had a feeling she didn't. She never told me any funny things or anything about how her shifts had gone.

I poured myself some orange juice and ate a bowl of

cereal. No milk. I couldn't stand milk, I didn't like the taste.

When I got to the theatre, I walked in to pots of paint of all colours in the backstage room. At least I'd get to play around a bit with colours. I found Freddy in the office, his head in his hand.

"Everything ok?" I asked sceptically.

"Our two main actors are late and we can't start without them. Well, I can't start without them. You're on set today so you're fine. Would you mind focusing on that today?" He asked, lifting his head to look at me.

"Of course." I shut the door behind me and headed to the room for set design. I pulled on a painting apron and had a look around. The room I was in was a huge box room, no windows, just a light on the ceiling. Cardboard templates made out the shapes of the castle, already painted and ready for the show. I decided to start with the first scene and began to put together a waterfall. I'd cut the cardboard out and was about to start painting when I heard the door open.

"Wow, you're really good!" Jake exclaimed.

"Thank you. Freddy's looking for you." I replied.

"I know, I'm hiding for a bit." He grinned.

"You'll get into trouble and set the production back." I fretted, picking up a paint brush and glancing at him. He brushed his hair away from his face and sat on the floor next to me. I ignored him and began the first coat of blue for the flowing water. I was using different tones and shades of blue so it looked like the water was flowing. The base of it would be harder, I'd never painted a brick pattern before. Jake cleared his throat.

"How long have you been doing this?" He asked.

"I studied art for four years."

"Wow. You're really talented. Can I help?" He tried to take the brush from my hand, causing my head to snap round. "I did art for a GCSE alongside drama." I couldn't help but notice his eyes sparkle.

"Ok, but stay I the lines I paint for you."

"Aww, it's like colouring when I was five." He laughed and I smiled. I painted the lines for the rest of the flowing water before passing him the paintbrush with the darker shade on it. He took it and contentedly started painting. Almost half an hour passed before Freddy bust in.

"Jake! Where the hell have you been?"

"Helping Addison paint. Prince Charming isn't in every scene you know." He winked at me.

"No, not every scene, but he is in the one we're trying to work on. Please come help us, you can help Addison in a bit, I don't need you for too long." He sighed.

"Ok." Jake began to get up. "Here you go Addy." I swear I felt a high voltage of electricity pulse through my veins as his fingers accidentally touched mine. I blushed as I took the brush from him. I felt something in me drop when he closed the door behind him.

No no no. No distractions. Not again. I'd gotten distracted by a boy at my last job and ended up fired. It was in retail which I hated anyway, but it was a job nonetheless. It still earned me money. I'd worked there for almost a year and he'd started three months before I was fired. I'd been asked to train him, which proved to be difficult when he kept looking at me with bright blue eyes behind his dark hair. He always wore a strong smelling aftershave and I always knew

21

when he was around. I watched my actions more when he was around so I didn't embarrass myself. We hung out often after shifts and went out for dinners regularly.

I'd been asked to set up a new display when Jamie walked past me. The strong waft of aftershave knocked me off my feet and I felt like I was up in the clouds. I wasn't. I ended up losing my footing on the ladder I was on, fell off and knocked down half the shelves on the aisle with me. My manager stormed over to me and sacked me on the spot. I completed the final hour of my shift and afterwards me and Jamie sat in the park. The sun was setting and we were lying in the basket swing together. His arms was wrapped around my shoulders, my head on his chest.

"I'll miss you on shifts." He whispered.

"Me too, but I'll still see you. I'm not moving away." I laughed, snuggling into him.

"I know."

It was that moment. My first kiss. At sixteen. My pulse was racing through my veins, my breath short. Jamie leaned his head to the side slightly and pressed his lips to mine ever so gently. He cupped my cheek with his hand and I put my hand on his shoulder. His lips caressed mine. It felt like fireworks were going off in the sky behind us. His body twisted to face me and he pulled me closer. I gasped as his tongue traced mine once before it pulled away. We were out of breath when we broke apart. The sun was setting, the birds flying into their trees.

It was over after our kiss. Jamie moved away to London just over a month later for college and he rarely answered my calls. It was after that that I promised I wouldn't fall in love again with someone I worked with. The aftermath was too painful.

I pulled my focus back to the flowing waterfall. After a couple more coats it would be perfect. I picked up the bottom bits and took off the lid of the grey paint. I was going to try grey stone bricks with moss and ivy. Fingers crossed it would look good. A few hours passed with nothing but me and my background music. I was about to stop for lunch when the door opened again.

"Hey, I got you lunch."

"Oh, thanks Jake. I didn't think you'd be done for another couple hours?" I could hear the confusion in my voice.

"I'm in all of five minutes of the scene they're working on. Lauren isn't doing too well today." He shrugged. I put my paintbrush into the pot and gratefully accepted the McDonald's he handed to me. "Thank you."

"I didn't know what you'd like, so I kind of got you chicken nuggets." I glanced at him and he looked sheepish.

"They're my favourite."

We sat on the floor and ate our food. I ate mine quickly because I needed to get back to work.

"Do you ever take breaks?" He laughed when I picked the brush back up.

"Only when I'm not the only set designer around. Besides, the more I do it, the quicker it'll be done."

"Then let me help." He put the rubbish in the bin and put on another apron. "I'll finish the water for you." He began adding more coats of paint to the water while I outlined the bricks for the bottom. I wanted it to be perfect. Jake seemed really happy I'd let him help me so I asked him to help on the bottom once he'd finished the coat he was doing.

"Do you fancy dinner tonight?" he asked.

"Where?" I asked, thinking whether it was a good idea to go against my rules.

"Anywhere you like." Wow. Freedom.

"Sure, we'll have a walk around later and choose somewhere."

"Ok."

I wasn't doing anything bad, was I? Colleagues go out for dinner together and drinks all the time. Nothing had to happen. It wasn't a date.

I was full of anxiety for the rest of the day. I couldn't stop wondering about dinner would end. I couldn't bear another work romance like mine and Jamie's, especially when he moved away and cut me off. It was agony.

It was relatively dark when we finished up for the day. I shivered into my jacket as we stepped into the cool evening air. Jake put his hand on the small of my back and guided me towards the top of the high street. We had a few decent pubs and restaurants near the theatre, I wondered which one he was taking me to.

"So do you know where you'd like to go?" He asked.

"Nope. You can choose."

"You sure?"

I nodded in response. We walked up towards the nicer pub, the more expensive one. Laughter radiated from inside. It was hot as we walked in. He put his hand on my back again and gently guided me to one of the far corners. We sat in a booth that was more closed off than the others.

The pub was painted green and gold for the interior. Paintings of various paraphernalia were hung up on the walls to add colour and decoration. The chairs in the booths were made from leather, the other sets of tables and chairs were wood. The floor was wooden floorboards, lamps hung around the walls. There was a bar near the entrance door to the pub and it was very crowded. I picked up the drink menu before passing it to him.

"What would you like?"

"A gin and lemonade please. Cherry gin if they have it." I requested.

He got up from the booth and made his way to the bar. My eyes dropped to his backside before flicking back up to look at the bar. So many thoughts were buzzing around in my mind, like bullets being shot. One straight after the other. I shook them off when I saw him walking back over carrying two drinks. I smiled as he placed my gin and lemonade on the table in front of me. I picked it up and took a sip.

A waitress came over to our table. Her hair was blond and short, she had brown eyes and her uniform was messy. She wasn't wearing it overly neatly. She was holding a pen and order pad.

"What would you like to eat?" She asked, looking at Jake. I could see the lust in her eyes and a blush was slowly spreading across her cheeks.

"I'd like a burger and chips please." Jake asked, his deep voice sending goosebumps up my arms.

"Sure." She replied, barely audible. "You?" She asked, but kept her eyes focused on Jake.

"Pasta please." She noted it down, took our menus and headed off to the kitchen.

I picked up my drink and had a few long sips from it. Jake had his eyes focused on mine as he waited for me to speak. I didn't. He cleared his throat.

"Set design seems fun." He pointed out.

"It is, it's the reason why I love being backstage. Everyone in the audience always thinks that the actors painted it when it's actually the people you never see during the performance. Being backstage is like the stitches in clothes, it keep it all together." I explained, feeling a little more confident.

"It sounds better than being onstage. I like being the lead actor because of the attention, but I'm never confident when I'm up there. I get ignored by my parents at home so theatre feels like the only way to get people to pay attention to me." His eyes clouded over as he spoke as if he was lost in thought.

"I'm sorry to hear about your family."

"Don't be, I'm used to it now." Jake sighed. "Tell me about you."

"What would you like to know?" I asked, the corners of my mouth lifting.

"Your interests, family life, career choice, hobbies. All of it."

"Well, at home it's just me and mum. My dad left us when I was little and he left mum to struggle. It became a regular sight to see unopened bill envelopes on the kitchen table because she couldn't bring herself to look at the amounts inside. So after leaving college last year, I got this job so I could help her pay the bills, although she hates that she's technically the reason why I got job straight out of college." I stopped talking as our waitress arrived with our food. Once again she kept her gaze fixed on Jake as she put our plates down.

"Anything else you'd like?" She asked him. Jake ordered another round of drinks for us both. She went to go get them.

"I think it's great that you're trying to help your mum

out. You're such a good daughter."
We talked and drank for about another hour before
we decided to call it a night. I was feeling tipsy and
wobbled slightly as I walked. Jake slipped his arm
around my waist as he slowly walked me home.
"Thanks for tonight." I slurred. " I loved you. It. I
meant I loved it."
He laughed softly. "I loved it too. Rain check for
another night?"
"Definitely."

CHAPTER 4

A few weeks passed and production was going well. Jake and I had been out for a couple more meals together, occasionally with Lauren and Vanessa. Tyler was becoming concerned about Lauren, she was becoming withdrawn. I'd gotten a lot more set ready and Jake had managed to memorise all of his lines. We were getting closer to our performance date and I needed to pull my focus back. It had strayed to constantly dreaming about Jake and it needed to stop. We'd blocked most of the scenes and were focusing on lighting. Costumes were being made, set almost completely finished. It was shaping together quite well. But the next Thursday morning, all hell broke loose.

"Lauren's quit!" Tyler cried. Everyone stopped what they were doing and turned to look at him. "She's called and said she's quitting. Now what are we going to do? Our lead actress is gone." He slumped into a chair. Jake nudged me forward.

"Addison is her understudy, she can do it." I was

going to kill him.

"Of course. Don't worry folks, crisis averted. Thanks Addison."

I felt my jaw drop. How could he do that to me? And why? He knew my fear of being onstage, I'd told him that during one of our nights out. Yet he had to go and backstab me. Prick. We went back to what we'd been doing before Tyler had burst in and I felt someone nudge my arm.

"At least now I get to kiss you." He whispered before walking away. Holy shit. Jake had done that because he wanted to kiss me. I felt the heart of a thousand burning stars course through me and I fully took in what he'd said. I really needed to finish memorising the lines. I wasn't convinced I'd be a good Cinderella. After a week of close contact with Jake onstage, I'd given up trying to stay away. If I fell for him, then so be it. I could already feel myself falling for him. How could anyone not?

"Dinner tonight?" He asked between scene transitions.

"I'll meet you outside the main entrance." I grinned. We were working on the final scene, the kiss scene. Tyler had suggested we work on the last few scenes as I'd watched the first being blocked.

Lady Tremaine descended the stairs. "Oh look daughters of mine, the prince is here!"

"I want to be a princess!" Anastasia wailed.

"No, me!" Shrieked her sister. There was a knock on the door. Both girls squealed in excitement. Lady Tremaine crossed the stage to the door and opened it to the Duke.

"Evening, by request of the Prince, all ladies of the household are required…" He began.

"Yes yes do come in."

Both girls were sat on the couch, waiting for their turn. In the meantime, Ella was locked in the basement, but able to hear each word.

"Oh I do wish there was a way out of here." I said as I began to pace back and forth. "They need to know it was I who danced with the prince, not my step sisters." I pretended to play with my skirt as the costumes weren't quite ready.

"Very good." Praised Freddy. "Then your animal friends give you the key they got from upstairs and you unlock the door from inside and rush upstairs to your Prince."

I unlocked the door and made my way to the sitting room to join my step-family.

"What on Earth are you doing?" My step mother yelled. "Oh ignore her my Prince, she's just our servant, she doesn't need a turn."

"Oh I believe she does." Jake replied and winked at me. I felt my face turn crimson. "Please, sit."

I sat down as instructed and lifted one leg over the other. Jake knelt in front of me and took off the shoe I was wearing. He slid on a white heel in its place. My step family gasped in shock.

"It fits! My Princess, I've found you. Come to the palace and be my Queen and rule with me."

I took a deep breath because I knew what was coming next.

"Of course I will!" I cried. Jakes hand slipped round my waist and pulled me in close to him.

"You're my happy ever after." He whispered and his lips softly brushed against mine. Adrenaline pulsed through me and I parted my lips slightly. His arm gripped me tighter and I lifted a hand to his chest. His smell was intoxicating, as was his kisses. His lips were so soft and gentle against mine. My fingers worked their way up into his hair and it did indeed feel as though it was happily ever after.

"Great work!" Shouted both Tyler and Freddy as they clapped.

"We'll rehearse the wedding scene as soon as Addison's dress is made." Said Freddy.

I looked up at Jake and he was looking at me. "I told you." He smiled. I blushed before Vanessa pulled me off the stage.

"Nora is after you for your fittings."

"Oh great."

Vanessa led me down a lot of hallways before we reached the Costume Design room. The door opened onto a room filled with various fabrics shelved on the walls. In the middle of the room was a wooden platform with a mirror behind it. Fabrics of floral patterns were strewn across the floor with an older lady scrabbling to pick them up.

"Hi Nora." Vanessa called. Nora looked up and smiled at us. "I've brought you Addison."

"Ah the princess to be." She laughed. "Come here darling, I just need your measurements for now." I waved goodbye to Vanessa and headed over to Nora.

"Where would you like me?" I asked.

"On the platform please my dear." I began to step up onto the platform but she stopped me. "I'll need you to be in your underwear dear so I can get the measurements right."

I slowly took my clothes off, keeping a watchful eye on the door. Who knew when someone might walk in?

"I lock the door during fittings." Nora said as though

she'd read my thoughts.

"Ok, thank you."

I stepped onto the platform, holding my arms around myself to try to keep warm. Nora moved to various positions around my body and I shivered every time her cold measuring tape touched the heat of my skin.

"Are you alright with strapless, dear? Tyler wants the wedding dress to be strapless."

"Yeah, I'm alright with them. Do the others have sleeves?" I asked in return.

"More or less." She responded. Her wispy grey hair kept flitting into her eyes. After around ten minutes, she walked back around to my front. "You're all done dear."

"Thanks Nora."

I jumped off the platform and pulled my jeans back on, trying to balance on one leg.

"Do you need me to grab anyone else for you?" I asked as I opened the door to leave.

"Not yet dear, you best get back before they send a search party." She laughed as I closed the door. I navigated my way back to where everyone else was waiting for me. A scarlet wave overtook my cheeks when I saw Jake. The kiss we'd shared before I went to Nora. I knew it was part of the performance, but the way he kissed me made me feel as though it was a little more than that. God only knew I couldn't wait to kiss him again.

I took myself off to do more set designing for the afternoon. They'd hired someone else for my old role so I wouldn't be drowning in my work, it had definitely lifted a weight off my shoulders. I knocked on the door.

"Yeah?"

"It's me."

"Oh, I suppose you can come in."

I laughed as I opened the door. Stefan was crouching on the floor, covered head to toe in paint a glitter. His blond hair was streaked with different colours and so was his face. His green eyes stood out against his pale skin.

"You look like something from a Picasso piece."

"Oi you cheeky bugger!" He shot back as he turned around to face me. I picked up another paint brush. He was working on the wedding scene, the set for the church already partially completed. The thing I'd begun to learn about Stefan was that he never worked in a logical order. Where I'd left him with the first four scenes done, he'd moved to making the pieces of set for the last few scenes.

"Do you want any help?" I asked.

"That would be great. Although shouldn't you be kissing Prince Charming?" He mocked.

"Jake. And no because I kissed him earlier." I giggled.

"I bet that got your tongue tied. He is rather easy on the eyes, isn't he?"

"Yes." I replied, feeling a blush stretching its way across my cheeks. My face was admitting to the crush I still needed to keep under wraps.

"Are your dresses pretty?"

"I haven't seen them. I've just had my dress measurements done so that Nora can begin to make them."

"I bet your wedding dress will be gorgeous."

"Me too." I felt myself beginning to daydream so I snapped my attention back the task at hand.

We finished for day quite early. It was Friday, Tyler's favourite, so that could've been why. I didn't feel like dinner with Jake tonight, I wanted time with mum. A girl's night in. Birds were scouring the streets for crumbs of food.

Mum was cooking when I arrived home. I locked the front door behind me and followed the smell into the kitchen.

"Hi mum." I said as I hugged her from behind.

"Oh hi sweetie. I wasn't expecting you yet, aren't you going out with Jake like you often do on Fridays?" She asked as she turned around and held me back.

"We finished earlier than I expected today and I don't fancy diner with Jake today. I would like a mother-daughter night." I proposed.

"We haven't done that in ages!" Mum exclaimed. "Let's cook dinner together and have a girly pamper night."

Mum and I made ourselves pasta. She fried the mince in an oiled saucepan whilst I cut the onions and carrots to mix in with it. Mum put the pasta into another saucepan with boiling water. I was careful with the knife I was using because our kitchen was tiny and mum kept walking to the sink to drain off the excess fat and oil. I added the onion, carrot and sweetcorn to the mince. Mum left me with the saucepan while she washed up in the sink. When the vegetables were cooked, I opened a jar of Bolognese sauce and tipped it in. I stirred it so that everything was coated in the sauce. Once the sauce was finished, I waited for the pasta. Two minutes left.

"I love cooking with you. We used to do it all the time when you were younger." She reminisced. The timer beeped so I moved the pasta to the sink and drained it through the sieve.

"Me too."

Mum had laid bowls out on the side so I dished up both our dinners. As mum poured some orange juice while I carried both bowls through to the living room. Mum put the glasses on the coffee table and put on the TV.

"Is the production going well, dear?" Mum asked.

"Yes, the scenes seem to be going quite well. We began working on the scene where she gets her shoe back and they kiss in happiness." Oops. I forgot I'd told her I was now Cinderella.

"Oh so you kissed Jake today then?" The cheeky smile she gave me the beginning of a blush to form.

"Yes." I said as I hung my head. Mum grinned like the Cheshire Cat, ear to ear. She made a weird squeak sound and I peered up at her. "Let's finish dinner and have a pamper night. No more questions about Jake or his kissing antics.

"No more questions about Jake and his kissing antics." Mum repeated.

CHAPTER 5

We spent the evening in my bedroom, doing facemasks and stuffing ourselves with popcorn. "Have they found a replacement for you yet? You can't be lead actress and backstage at the same time; they're both very time demanding roles." Mum asked, concern in her eyes.

"Yes, someone called Stefan. He's lovely. When I'm not needed anywhere then I sneak away and do set design." She smiled in response and began to peel off her face mask.

It was after ten when mum suggested I go to bed.

"Goodnight mum."

"Goodnight sweetie."

When I was tucked in bed, my mind drifted off to how Jake had kissed me. How soft his lips were, how caring. How gentle he was when he'd held onto me. Was I excited for him to kiss me again? Did it mean anything if it's just a performance rehearsal?

A week later, I wished I'd been ten minutes later

getting there than I was. If I'd been late, I wouldn't have heard the conversation I had. The conversation that had led to me crying in the backstage toilets.

I arrived at the theatre before most people. I was early, ridiculously early. I was walking to the dressing rooms to talk to Nora when I saw two people talking around the corner. I took a few steps backwards before they saw me.

"What on earth do you mean? She's doing great given the circumstances." One voice said sharply. Jake.

"She's not fit for the part. Or pretty. She should be behind the scenes, unseen from everyone where she belongs." A female voice. I knew that the actress of one of the sisters was praying to earn the Cinderella role once Lauren had quit, but I'd got it instead.

"Addison had no reason to be Cinderella."

"No, Tyler and Freddy are loving her performance though. She has earned everything she's got from here."

"She's not good enough, Cinderella's supposed to be pretty, that's why she becomes a princess." I had a feeling it was the actress of Anastasia with him. I peeked round the corner and saw them stood closely together. Jake was backing against a wall as she walked closer to him. She put her hand on his shoulder. "I bet she's not even a good kisser."

He threw her hand off him. "Get off."

She drew even closer, their chests almost touching. "If I'd got the part, I could make you feel so much more than her. I'd kiss you so gently," She pressed him against the wall. "Then after the show, I'll take you home. Back to my place, strip you down and we'd fuck late into the night. You'd make me scream your name over and over…"

I never heard the rest, or Jake's reply. I turned around and sprinted at full speed to the toilets. Which was how I ended up locked in one crying for however long. I lost track of time. Tears flooded down my cheeks, the wetness blurring my vision. I sat curled up on the floor in the stall I'd locked myself into. I knew Jake had defended me, but she'd pushed it way too far.

I was alerted shortly later on by someone calling my name.

"Addison?"

I sniffled and didn't respond. The bathroom door opened. "Addy? Oh Addy are you ok?" So she'd seen the closed cubicle door then. "Honey open the door." I slid back the lock on the door and Vanessa pushed it open slightly. Seeing my face, she walked into the cubicle and pulled me in for a hug. "Everyone's waiting for you."

"Ok." I wiped my nose at the back of her sleeve and peered up into Vanessa's concerned eyes. Her hair was up in a ponytail with a small plait running through part of it. She held out her hand and I took it as I heaved myself up.

"We'll clean you up and then we'll go in." Vanessa led me to the sink and began running cold water from the taps. It trickled out slowly at first. She wetted some of the handtowels stored above the sinks and slowly washed my face. The coolness of the water cooled down the swelling and puffiness of my eyes after all my crying. I dried my face on my sleeve.

"Let's go." I gave her my best smile.

"That's the spirit, Addy."

We walked side by side to the main room of the theatre. Everyone's attention snapped to us as we opened the doors. Jake's expression conveyed shock. "Are you all right?" Freddy asked as he began to get up.

"Yes I'm fine," I croaked, "Please stay sat and carry on."

I sat in the row in front of Jake. I could feel his eyes staring into my skull from behind. I concentrated on Freddy. Tyler didn't appear to be present this morning.

"We won't be doing any scenes today. With Tyler not here today or tomorrow, we'll all be focusing on our costumes and set design. Stefan and Addison can help if you have questions for the set pieces. Nora will call for people throughout the day for fittings or measurements and anything regarding your costumes. We've told her how we'd like them, but Tyler and I agreed to give you a little freedom to make a couple changes." Freddy paused. "Vanessa I'd like your prompts and views on lighting. Everyone else to set design please. It needs completed. Thank you."

We all got up and went to set design. I found my piece from the wedding scene I'd started and Jake joined me. I remained silent until he spoke.

"Are you alright? I saw you crying earlier." "His voice sounded thick with worry. Did I tell him what I saw or did I just leave it? Before I could comment Anastasia came over.

"Hey Jake," She purred, her voice filled with lust. She began to wrap a hand round his neck but he swatted it down. "Wanna paint with me?"

It looked as though he glared at her. "No Tara, I'd rather stay with Addy. Work with Stefan." Jake turned around so he was completely opposite me and his back was to her. Tara huffed before storming away.

Again.

"I saw you two earlier." I said out of the blue a few moments later.

Jake ran his hand through his hair. "Did you? Did you hear anything?"

"I did. I heard you defending me and shutting her insults towards me down; I thank you very much for that. I also saw her push you to the wall and saying what she'll do to you…" I trailed off.

"So you didn't see me push her off and say my heart is elsewhere?" He questioned, looking at me dead in the eyes.

"No, I saw that and ran away after deciding I'd seen enough." I focused back on my work. He lifted my chin with his little finger.

"It lies with you." I felt my jaw almost drop.

"M-me?" I stammered.

"Yes. I've like you since our first meal out. You might not have, but I saw every meal out when it was just us as a date." Jake confessed.

"You did?" I asked, doubt creeping into my tone.

"Yes." He explained, exasperated, as he ran another hand through his hair.

"Oh." Our eyes locked, I slowly released a breath.

"Addison and Jake." We both turned our heads to find Nora holding a clipboard and pen. She had a measuring tape draped around her shoulders and was wearing a blue cotton dress. "Can you come try on your final scene costumes please? Stylists are waiting." Jake and I stood up and followed Nora to the dressing rooms. It was a huge room with mirrors and chairs in stations down one side. Clothes rails were along the far back wall. I took a peek at all the costumes and gasped at Cinderella's wedding dress.

The dress was like a ball gown. It was strapless, the bodice made with silk and little flowers were embroidered into it. The skirt was tulle and flowed out around the bottom; it was gorgeous. I couldn't believe I would be wearing something as beautiful as that dress. No way would that look good on me, I thought.

"Dressing rooms are behind you both." Said one of the stylists. Her hair was in a pixie cut and was dyed in two colours: half pink and half blue.

"Thank you." Jake and I said in unison.

"Would you like help changing dear? The dress might be difficult for you to do up." Suggested Nora.

"Please."

Jake went into one changing room as I followed Nora into another. She carried my dress as though it belonged to a queen, gently and gracefully. She undid the dress while I took my jeans and top off. She placed the dress gently on the floor and I carefully stepped into it. We pulled it gently up my body and I twisted around so she could do up the back. I was in awe at the pattern on the bodice. The dress pushed my boobs up a bit, I wasn't sure if it was good or not. Nora pulled back the dressing room curtain and I stepped out and walked to the styling chairs.

Jake was already changed into his navy blue tux. He was jaw-dropping gorgeous at that moment.

"You have such beautiful hair." Pixie girl said as she brushed through it. She brushed all the knots out before plugging in a curling iron. My eyes opened wider, I didn't like my hair curly. "Don't worry, I'm only going to curl the ends and see how that looks."

I nodded meekly.

Keeping my head still and straight for as long as I did

was painful. I wanted to steal peeks at Jake but couldn't without my stylist complaining. After an hour, we were done with my hair. A tiara was placed upon my head with a long veil attached to it. I got up and looked at myself in the full height mirror.

"Wow, you look beautiful." Jake said, coming up behind me. "You really look like a princess in the wedding dress, Nora did an amazing job." He rested his hand on my hips and I sucked in a breath. My hair was down, curls on my shoulders.

"You do look rather handsome. " I blushed as I pulled my hair over one shoulder.

"Thank you."

Nora took a picture of us both in our costumes and then asked us to change. We changed back into our normal clothes and then began walking the long walk to the set design room. Jake clasped my hand unexpectedly and I gasped. I looked up into his eyes and watched his smile from ear to ear.

"You are really, very beautiful." Jake took a step towards me. His eyes dropped to my lips for just a second and I parted them. Slipping a hand round my waist, he slowly lowered his lips to mine. I felt my body ignite as he kissed me. I rested a hand on his shoulder, another round his neck. We drew back for breath for just a second and then he pulled me back in. I felt his tongue trace my lower lip and my mouth opened a little wider, just enough for him to slip his tongue in. My body shivered in shock at the touch. I pulled away.

"We need to go. We should be working." I whispered, his nose touching mine and our lips almost locking again.

"They won't even know we aren't there." He flirted,

placing a delicate kiss on my nose.

"Mm Tara will."

"I don't care for Tara. She's obsessive, been after me for the whole three years since I met her, yet she continues to ignore me when I say I'm not interested." He laughed and I let out a small laugh too. Our faces were still touching.

"It still hut to see this morning though."

"Would you rather you were in her place at that moment?" He pressed his lips to mine again. I nodded slightly when he drew back. "Thought you might." He grinned.

"Let's get going."

Jake laughed and let me through to the room with everyone else. I went back to the wedding flowers I'd been drawing. I was making arches with leaves and roses. I was going to put glitter on the roses so that they would stand out in the lighting. If Jake didn't keep distracting me, then my vision would be perfect if it looked as good as it did in my head. Tara was glaring at us from her corner with Stefan. I smiled back at her.

I sketched out the design of the roses and the leaves. At the moment, it looked like random lines and zigzags. I got a big pair of scissors and began cutting around the outer leaves that made the arch shape. I then mixed some paint together to create a light shade of green. I painted the leaves as Jake painted another set piece. I waited for the green to begin to dry slightly before paining the roses. I coloured the red and pink on the tips of each petal.

Hours passed before everyone had finished. I was sure it was late evening. We all filed out of the theatre, finished for the day. Jake swept up behind me and took my hand. He led me up the high street and I assumed we were going for dinner. I was filled with confusion when we walked past the pub.

"Where are we going?" I asked becoming increasingly more confused.

"To the club."

"Oh?"

It was loud when we arrived, the sound of the bass music could be heard from three roads away. A long queue of people were lined up at the door, two very large, tall men stood outside dressed in full black.

"Jake, are you sure about this?"

"Yes, trust me Addy, it'll be fine. You do have you ID with you though, right?"

"I never leave home without it."

"Good."

We joined the back end of the line to go in. The music was really loud, would I really enjoy this like he seemed to think? When we eventually reached the front of the line, the bouncers stamped our left hands and allowed us in. Bright lights and even louder music awaited us inside.

"I'll get us drinks, what would you like?"

"I'll come with, it's too crowded for me to feel safe left alone." I followed him up to the bar.

"What will it be?" Asked the bartender.

"Rum and coke." I asked as I looked at Jake.

"Two rum and cokes." Jake requested. I watched with curiosity as the bartender made up our drinks. He was so swift in making them and barely spilt a drop. He handed them both to Jake and we left the bar. We took a table at the edge of the dancefloor and drank our drinks.

"Productions going well." He stated.

"Yes it is. It's only three weeks until our opening performance. I'm really anxious."

"Don't be."

"Why?"

"Because you're perfect for the role, you deserve the role. You're a perfect Cinderella." I smiled, a blushing spreading across my cheeks. He took my hand. "You have nothing to worry about."

We drank a few more drinks and then made our way to the dancefloor. Taylor Swift was playing and Jake took my hand and made me sway to the music. Bright blue and pink lights circulated the room. We danced our way through lots of songs before Jake slightly pulled back.

"I'm going to the toilets. Keep dancing and I'll come back."

I watched as Jake walked towards the toilets and I took to the floor again. I wasn't dancing much, I didn't want to embarrass myself whilst I was alone. Two hands held onto my hips and I picked up speed thinking Jake had returned. Soft kisses were laid on my neck with hot breath soothing my skin. I wrapped his hands around my waist and pressed my back against his chest.

"Well aren't you getting down." A gruff voice slurred in my ear. I instantly dropped his hands and turned to look at the guy. He had blond hair and hazel eyes, eyes that were glazed over. I tried to step away from him but he held onto my wrists tightly. "Where are you going, babe? I'm not done yet."

"Please let me go." I said, trying to pull myself away again. He tightened his grip.

"Let her go!" Thank God Jake was back. Jake wrapped a protective arm around me.

"She your girl?" The stranger asked.

"Yes." Jake replied.

"Sorry mate, didn't know." He said and walked away. Jake turned to me, his eyes searching mine. "You ok?"

"I am now thanks."

"Drink?"

"Please."

I was more than drunk by the time we left. I couldn't walk straight, Jake held my waist the whole way out the club. We were both drunk, me more than him.

"Can't go home." I slurred, tripping slightly. "Mum will kill me."

"Stay at mine." Jake pounced.

"Ok."

We slowly made our way to Jake's flat. The moon shone down on us, basking us in a silver glow. His flat was small, a one bedroom place. His lips were on mine as soon as he'd closed the door. I tangled my fingers in his hair and pulled gently, receiving a soft moan in response. His tongue traced my lips. I gently bit his lip and felt electricity surge through my veins. He picked me up by my thighs and I instinctively wrapped my legs around his waist. He carried me through to his bedroom.

Jake's room was clean, for a guy. The walls were blue, he carpet grey and a double bed was on the far wall. He threw me onto his bed and I giggled.

He climbed on the bed, on top of me, and placed slow, gentle kisses down my neck. His hot breath was making my skin start to tingle.

"You're so hot baby." He groaned.

I felt myself begin to pant under his touch.

I was starting to feel myself sobering up as I lay on

the bed, closed my eyes briefly and discovered the room didn't start spinning.

His hand slipped under my shirt and began exploring my bare skin underneath. With the other hand he lifted my shirt up over my head. His eyes popped as he took in the sight of me in my bra on his bed. His lips crashed down on mine and he began unzipping my jeans. Pulling them down, he moved and kissed down the length of my thighs and I moaned with every hot kiss and my back arched off the bed. He threw my jeans to the other side of the room. I sat up and pulled off his shirt and he grazed his lips against my chest. I felt pressure begin to build in my lower stomach. I pulled him up and our lips locked.

He pushed me back and took his jeans off so he was wearing nothing. I laid myself back down on the bed. I gasped as I saw how ready he was for me, so so ready. His fingers stroked down my stomach and slipped under my pants. Gently he pulled them down. My breath quickened my pulse racing through my veins.

"Oh Addy, you're so gorgeous." He moaned as he kissed my stomach. I winced at the pain of him slipping a finger inside me. He repeatedly laid kisses on my thighs and I found myself filled with such a level of pleasure that I had never before felt in my life.

"I want you Jake." I whispered.

"Ok baby," he purred, "You can have me." He pulled my pants completely off and lifted me higher up towards the pillows. He climbed on top again and I felt his want for me press into my thigh. I was as ready for him as he was for me.

I needed him.

Reaching inside his bedside drawer, I heard the sound of foil. *Oh shit.* He took it between his teeth and tore it open. I averted my gaze to the ceiling as I felt him roll the condom on before pressing his lips to my neck.

This was it.

He stroked me before I felt him slip inside me. A wave of pleasure took me over and then a tiny sting of pain. My body was remembering this feeling from years ago.

He was so slow, so gentle. He was caressing every inch of skin, every little part of my body as he kissed me all over. I'd never been touched like this before, not by any other guy I'd dated. Jake was so intimate with every touch he laid on my body, every searing hot kiss he gave me.

We fit each other perfectly like two puzzle pieces.

I moaned as he pulled himself out a little before strongly pushing back in.

"Is this ok?" He panted. I didn't say anything, I just gazed into his eyes and nodded.

His lips locked on mine and I opened my mouth so he could taste me. His tongue played with mine as his hand pressed down on my stomach. Holy shit, the things he was making me feel. He pressed down on my stomach, making me squirm and moan and the pressure that became more intense. My eyes rolled to the back of my head.

"I can feel you getting tighter." He moaned in my ear. He began to pick up his pace of sliding in and out of me. I bit my lip, trying to hide my pleasure. His lips grazed my neck and he sucked it gently and I was done. I felt myself come undone all over him. He moaned loudly in my ear.

He thrust himself into me harder, causing me to whimper. I watched the muscles on his shoulder strain.

"That was amazing." He panted. I stroked my fingers through his hair, his sweaty face pressed to the soft skin on my chest. I smiled and gazed up at him. He wrapped an arm round my shoulder and we closed our eyes and fell asleep.

CHAPTER 6

I woke up in a strange bed. Where was I? I heard a
grunt next to me. Cautiously I looked next to me.
Memories from the previous night flooded my brain
as I saw Jake next to me. I remembered how we'd
ended the night. My blushing increased as Jake rolled
over and his face rested on my shoulder. I carefully
got out from the bed and covered myself with my
hands. I found my clothes strewn across different
parts of the room. My head was pounding from the
alcohol from last night.

 I padded through the flat to Jake's kitchen and put
the kettle on to boil. Looking around, I found a small
pot of hot chocolate and put a few spoonfuls into a
mug. I poured in the boiled water in and stirred.
Topping it with squirty cream from the fridge and sat
in the living room. After watching TV for a bit, I
heard the bedroom door open. Jake yawned and met
my eyes. His hair was dishevelled and his eyes
sparkled the sunrise at new dawn. Beautiful. He'd put
oxers and a t-shirt on before leaving the bedroom.

"I was surprised to find you weren't still lying next me when I woke up. Are you ok?" He asked as he sat beside me.

"Yeah I'm fine, I just needed a drink. Would you like me to make you one?"

"You're in my flat Addy, I should've made for you because you're the guest." He deadpanned.

"I don't mind honestly." I really didn't mind, but it felt nice that he wanted to do things for me. He got up and boiled the kettle again. He made a coffee, black, and came and sat back next to me. He wrapped an arm around my shoulders and I snuggled into him slightly. Then his phone rang.

"Hello?" He asked.

"It's Freddy. You don't need to come in today, Tyler's still off and I've got a stomach bug. I'll call everyone else and let them know." Freddy's voice croaked down the line.

"No need to call Addison, she's here with me so I'll tell her." Jake smiled at me.

"Ok, enjoy your day off."

He put the phone down.

"What was that?" I asked.

"We have a day off. Freddy's sick and Tyler isn't in either. So we can spend the day together again." He purred and leant closer so his lips met my nose.

"I'm down for that." I grinned.

"Great!" He lips met mine and I felt myself melt into the kiss. His arm held my tightly around my waist, keeping me close to him. I lifted and hand to his shoulder. We broke apart to catch our breath.

"What would you like to do today?" He asked, stroking my cheek.

"Something fun." I responded. He placed a kiss on

my forehead before retreating into the bedroom, presumably to get dressed.

I wondered to myself what today would bring as I took another sip of my drink. His coffee was still steaming on the floor by my feet. He didn't have a coffee table. Maybe he was treating today like a date? If he was, I was even more excited for today.

Jake came back out some time later, hair wet and fully dressed. He was a sight to behold. I felt myself falling further for him, even though I hated to admit it. Last night I'd felt more alive than I had since I could remember. Feeling his hot skin against mine, feeling how much he lusted for me through kisses… It had been blissful. Last night had been perfect, a night I'd think of for ages. I wanted to live another night like it, but did Jake? Had it meant as much to him as it had for me? I turned my attention back towards Jake.

"Are you ready?" He asked.

"Where are we going?"

"Hop in my car and find out." Winked Jake.

I picked up my phone from the sofa, put my shoes on and followed Jake into the lift. The doors closed and we were alone. We didn't utter a word the whole ride down.

It was a gorgeous bright morning. Clouds were dotted through the sky, the wind casted a gentle breeze. Jade green leaves from the branches, the crisp smell of morning filling the air. Birds flew around, people walked dogs and cars drove by.

Jake produced a set of car keys from his pocket.

"This one." He said as he pointed to a red Audi. The paint on the car sparkled in the sunlight. It looked almost brand new. He unlocked it and opened the passenger door for me.

"Wow." I gasped.

The seats were leather and carried its distinct scent with it. The car had a masculine feel about it. He had a jelly bean air freshener hanging from his rear view mirror. I clipped my seatbelt in and he started up the engine.

"I never knew you could drive." I acknowledged.

"That's because I'm within walking distance of work and I like the exercise. I don't tend to drive unless it's a long journey."

"So this is going to be a long car ride?" I asked as he gently reversed out of the parking space he was in. He turned left onto the main road and we were off on our little adventure. He hadn't told me where we were going and I was so tempted to ask. I gave in.

"Where are we going?"

"A place you told me you've always wanted to go to."

Well that narrowed it down, but not by much. There were lots of places I wanted to go. But which one was he taking me to?

"Hmm." I thought absent-mindedly. "That could be Devon, Brighton and Cornwall. Lots of places. Do I get a hint?"

"Not at all Addy. Nice try." Jake laughed.

A short time later I think I must've fallen asleep from the relaxed pace on the road. I opened my eyes and saw a sign that said Brighton in ten miles.

"Brighton!"

"Oh so you're awake now."

"Sorry." I yawned.

"It's ok, we were up later last night than you're probably used to."

"Yeah, but I wouldn't change it for the world." I whispered.

"What was that?"

"I said that yeah I'm not used to late nights like last night."

"Ok, we're not far now."

"Good because I need to pee."

"Want me to stop somewhere?" He asked.

"I can hold it until we stop, keep driving."

He changed lanes on the motorway and hit the accelerator. I opened my window and we were hit by the wind as we wove our way through other cars. I felt a feeling of freedom with Jake. Not just when I was in his car, but when I was simply spending time with him.

I felt free to do whatever I wanted to when I was with him. I looked back to last night. I wouldn't have done that with anyone else, I didn't have the self-confidence but I had thought that another guy would take one look at me and walk away. Jake had so gentle, so intimate. *Too intimate.* He'd made me feel things I'd never felt before. Last night was a night I'd treasure for a long time.

Jake and I arrived in Brighton and it took a long time to find a place to park. He began to find "Just Keep Swimming" as I watched him slowly become wound up by how busy it was. I was going to say something, but then changed my mind because I didn't think he'd find it helpful. I watched his frown turn into a grin as he found an empty spot. A little dimple showed, something I'd never noticed before.

We got out the car and I was in awe. We could see the beach from where we'd parked. It was so sandy, the ocean a bright blue and I couldn't wait to cover my toes in the sand.

Noticing my smile, Jake asked "Where first baby?"

I felt my heart skip a beat at him calling me "baby."
"Not sure, beach looks gorgeous though." I began taking careful steps in its direction.
"Like you."
I felt myself blush uncontrollably.
"Race you!" I called and took off running.
"Not fair, you had a head start!"
We ran through the people on the pavement. Some sent me confused looks but I didn't care. He'd remembered a place I'd always wanted to visit and he'd driven us the couple hour drive to get here. I was so happy. I saw him catching up as I looked out the corner of my eye so I increased my pace as the pavement became empty in front of me.
"I'm gonna win." I chanted, grinning ear to ear.
I did, in fact, win.
"Oh no. I lost." He laughed.
"Yep, and you owe me an ice cream as a reward to me for winning."
Jake rolled his eyes. "Fine. But I'm getting myself one. You can have a double scoop. I need to cool off after that running."
"Deal."
We wandered down the beach. The sand was soft between my toes; I'd taken off my shoes after our race. I felt the sun radiate its heat on my chest. Jake reached out my hand and slowly hooked his fingers between mine. My fingers twitched but I held onto his hand. My hair was a mess after running, my forehead was beaded with sweat. Jake's hair was wind-blown and his skin glowed.
We eventually came to a little café on the beach. It was just off the esplanade, it's foundation on the sand. It had a patio spreading out onto the sand with

a couple of table on it with the sun umbrellas up. A few people were sat outside, more queued up at the ice cream window. The café had small windows and not much room inside. It appeared to be mostly ice cream and beers. We joined the queue for ice cream. "Still allowed two scoops?" I asked, swaying myself side to side in plea.

"Yes."

"I wonder what flavours. I hope they hope they have my favourite."

"And what would that be?" He asked, raising his eyebrows at me.

"Cherry and chocolate."

"I'm not a fan of cherries, but that sounds lovely."

I took a glimpse at the ice cream cabinet. There were so many. Bubblegum, candyfloss, cherry bakewell, rhubarb and custard, parma violet; the lost went on. I hadn't knew half of them were ice cream flavours. Surprised, I said "There's so many."

"Well you can pick two or one."

"Definitely two." Who knew an eighteen year old could be so excited by ice cream? I didn't, but I clearly was excited. I felt like a child when your parents take you into a sweet shop. So many choices, but not allowed everything you see. I wasn't paying attention to anything until I felt Jake nudge my ribs. I stepped forward.

"A scoop of mint please." Requested Jake. He looked at me.

"A double scoop for me please. One cherry bakewell, the other rhubarb and custard please."

The lady behind the counter scooped up Jake's, put it in a cone and passed it to him.

"Cone or tub?" She asked me.

"Uhh tub please."

She passed mine a minute later. Jake handed over the cash and we thanked her as we left. I took a spoonful of cherry bakewell and slid it into my mouth. My mouth came alive at the sudden burst of cherry flavour. There were broken biscuit pieces in it too. I took a spoonful of rhubarb and custard. My tongue tingled at the sourness of the rhubarb but it then relaxed as the sweetness of the custard stole the sour taste away. I loved it. I loved them both.

I peeked up to Jake to see him biting away at his. Mint. Such a classic flavour for a guy to have.

"Shall we sit on the beach?" He asked.

"Please."

Jake found a vacant bench a little farther down the beach. Moment after I'd finished my ice cream, he took my face in his hands and kissed me. I felt fireworks go off like I had last night. Everything was perfect. I sucked in a breath and put my hand on his neck. I took his bottom lip between mine and gently sucked before letting go. It drove him crazy, I felt him tense beneath my touch.

He stroked my cheek and kissed my nose, my lips. His face was close to mine, his breath against my chin. I leant forward slightly and kissed him gently before he took my hand and led me down the beach.

Was I starting to fall in love with Jake?

CHAPTER 7

The sun stayed out all day. My excitement rocketed up as I found an arcade. Jake was taking photos of the beach as we walked. I slowly sneaked backwards whilst he wasn't looking and crept towards the arcade. "Jake!" I called, unable to bear him thinking he'd lost me. "I'm going to the arcade I found." I said as he jogged to catch up to me.

"Go for it. I'll meet you in there."

I jogged briskly to the arcade. It was massive. 2p machines, claw machines and child games filled the massive room. In a closed off part was the eighteen and above gambling machines. I had no interest in going on those.

I searched the claw machines to see if there was anything I wanted to win. I came to one with cuddly animals in it. A white fluffy polar bear caught my eyes and I set my target. I inserted a few pounds and made my attempts to catch it. It dropped it a few times near the prize drop box but it never fell in. A hand landed round my waist.

"Which one you going for?" Purred Jake.

"The polar bear. The stupid thing keeps dropping it." I huffed. I tried again and it almost made it. I threw my hands up in exasperation.

"Let me try. Take a tenner out my pocket and go on a different game." Jake said as he took my position at the machine controls.

"Which pocket?"

"Back." Oh.

"Ok."

I slipped my hand into his back pocket and I felt him tense beneath my touch. I slowly took my hand out his pocket once I'd gripped the only note in there and stroked him with the back of my hand as I took my hand out his pocket. I turned around and just about felt him leave a quick kiss on the back of my head.

I wandered over to all the 2p machines in the middle of the arcade. Most of them had keyrings inside, some had little toys in. I found one that had keyrings saying "I heart Brighton" on them. I searched around for a money converter machine and converted the tenner pound coins, and the five pounds into 2ps.

I began playing for the keyring and was surprised when I shortly caused an avalanche.

"Yes!" I cried and blushed as Jake looked over to me with a grin on his face. Bless him, he was still trying to win me the polar bear.

An hour passed in which I'd won two Brighton keyrings; one for each of us to remind us of today. Mine was already attached to my house keys. I went back to find Jake.

"I have three quid of yours back." Jake was focused on the claw, still holding the polar bear, dragging over to the prize box. It didn't drop it. We both jumped with joy. Jake leant down to pick it up.

"I believe this is yours." He held it out to me.

I hugged him. "Thank you so much!" I took it from him and cuddled it to my chest.

"Are you going to name it?"

"At some point, when I think of the perfect name." I suddenly remembered the keyring. "Oh yeah," I said as I fumbled around in my pocket. "This is for you. I have one as well and I thought we could both have one to remind us of today. I got it in the 2p machine."

He took it gratefully. "Thank you Addy." We looked into each other's eyes longingly. My stomach growled.

"What time is it?" I asked as I clutched my monster roaring stomach. Jake took out his phone and peered at the time.

"Time to get dinner and then drive back home. Shall we?" He asked, holding out his arm and putting on a posh accent.

"We shall." I giggled, taking his arm.

We looked on Google maps to find a nice place for dinner after leaving the arcade. There was one that looked good about ten minutes away. Jake led the way towards the centre.

I knew I was lucky. I was lucky to have been treated the way Jake had been treating me and he'd made me feel special. Some people don't ever get to experience the fireworks moments I'd been having and I was so grateful to have them.

The sun was beginning to set, the orange and pink colours in the sky creating a beautiful pattern. I was in awe. I'd had a perfect day. I'd ticked a place off my bucket list. Even though we'd spent the day on the

beach and in an arcade, it had still been perfect.
The pub we ended up at was called The Frog and
Mouse. It was an unusual name. We went in and
found a small table tucked in the corner by the bar. I
wouldn't be having alcohol tonight. The carpet was
red, the bar was big and well stocked. It was fancier
than your regular pub, polished tables, fluffy carpet,
expensive paintings on the walls.
I leant forward in my seat and picked up the menu
before Jake had a chance to. I watched as he slouched
in his seat while my eyes scanned the menu. I made
my selection before passing it to Jake. After a few
moments he beckoned the barmaid over.
Her brown hair was plaited and tied into a bun on her
head. She was dressed in all black.
"What can I help you with?" She asked politely.
"We're ready to order our food and we'd like two
lime sodas please." Oh did we now Jake? I couldn't
remember telling him what drink I'd like.
"Of course, I'll send someone over for your food
order."
"Thank you." I said. I stared across the table at Jake,
who was grinning like the Cheshire Cat with his little
dimple showing. Our waitress was blonde and she
had blue eyes. Her hair was in a ponytail.
"What can I get you both?" Her eyes were focused on
Jake.
Jake gestured to me. "Ladies first."
I cleared my throat. "I'd like tomato pasta with a side
of garlic bread please."
"Yep." She said, her attention still fully on Jake.
"You?"
"Steak please. Medium rare. With chips."
"Is that all?" She batted her eyelashes at him. I sat

smugly in my seat, safe in the knowledge his attention was on me.

"Yes." He said and she took our order through to the kitchen. The barmaid returned with our drinks.

"If you'd like another drink, call me over."

Jake smiled. "Thanks."

After she left, we sat in silence again. Why did it feel like there was tension in the air now? We'd spent all together in blissful happiness but now we were doomed to silence for dinner. What was going on? I shifted in my seat and turned my focus to the paintings. Most of them looked pre historic, some were from battles. They all looked expensive, that was one thing I was positive about.

"I've enjoyed today." Jake said, cutting into my thoughts.

"So have I." I replied, turning back around to face him.

"It's been special because it's been with you."

I didn't get to respond because the blond waitress bought our food over. She laid them on the table and stopped to stare at Jake. He gave her what, to me, looked like a glare and she skulked away.

"Bon appetite." He smiled, holding up his fork.

I stabbed at my pasta and took a mouthful. The flavours were strong and intense. And hot. Too hot. My tongue was on fire. I started choking and had to launch my hand at my lime soda. The cool liquid put the fire out. I looked across at Jake, my eyes watering.

"Oh don't worry, I'm fine." I wiped at my eyes.

"I know."

I rolled my eyes at him and picked up more pasta, this time blowing it. I dipped my garlic bread into the sauce once I'd eaten all the pasta. Jake had finished

before me and struggled to hold in his laughter when
I looked at him.

"What?" I snapped.

"You have sauce on your face." He leaned forward
and wiped tomato sauce from round my mouth with
his thumb. I watched intently as he sucked the sauce
off his thumb. I picked up my drink and downed the
rest of it.

"Dessert?" I asked, leaning towards the menu.

He snatched it away. "When we get home."

He walked over to the bar to pay the bill. In the
meantime, I got myself ready to leave.

"I'll meet you at the car." I called. I didn't know if he
heard me, I hoped he had. I waited by the Audi, my
arms around my body to keep warm. The car
unlocked and I got in.

Jake had the radio on the whole ride home. Music
filled the car to take away the unwanted silence. Once
we got on the motorway, Jake put his hand on my
thigh and squeezed it gently. Butterflies erupted in my
stomach.

"Are you staying at mine tonight or am I dropping
you home?"

"I'd like to stay at yours please." I saw him smile.

It felt the ride home was longer than it actually was.
We just about made it into the elevator before I had
his lips on mine. I smiled against his lips. I pressed
one gentle kiss to his lips and stepped back.

"Addy." He groaned.

"Wait."

"Fine." He took my hand. He crashed his lips on
mine again once he'd closed the flat door. This time I
didn't resist. I parted my lips for him, giving him
more of me to kiss. He scooped me up and took me

into his room. He gently placed me on the bed, not breaking this kiss. His hand stroked my waist, my fingers in his hair. He was knelt in front of me. His hand snuck beneath my shirt and he pulled it off. Jake trickled a trail of kisses from my ear, to my neck, to my collarbone.

"Jake." I gasped.

"It's just kisses, don't worry. Not like last night." His lips went past my chest and to my stomach. I felt the butterflies coming back. I yawned. Jake looked up at me.

"You're tired, we'll go to sleep."

"But I was enjoying that." I sighed.

"I saw you yawn. We have work tomorrow anyway." He got up off the door and left the bedroom. I heard the bathroom door close. Did I just ruin that? Had I upset Jake? Pushing my negative thoughts aside, I took my jeans off and climbed into the bed. Jake came back a few minutes later in his boxers and switched off the light. I turned onto my side so I would be facing away from him. Something thumped into the bed.

"Oof."

"There's a bed there." I stated.

"Thanks Addy, I had no idea." Jake laughed. I heard him patting his way up the bed until he found the pillows. He settled into bed behind me. I snuggled myself up under the duvet. Jake shifted to get comfortable.

"Addison?"

"Yes?" I whispered.

"Can I hold you?"

"If you wish."

Jake snaked his arm around me and I moved back

slightly so we were touching. My ass was on his stomach, his bare chest hot against my back. He wound his hand up to my chest and rested it there. I sucked in a breath. He must have noticed because he dropped his hand to my stomach. My breathing evened out. I felt his hot breath on the back of my neck.

I turned over to face him. I smiled into the darkness and brushed my nose to his.

"Don't push it." He murmured.

"I'm not."

"Trust me baby, you are."

Did I want to do this? The answer was a firm yes. I stroked his cheek and left a gentle kiss at the corner of his mouth. His jaw stiffened. His hand gripped onto me tighter. I placed a delicate kiss on his chest. I rolled onto my back and closed my eyes.

CHAPTER 8

I was woken up the next morning to something
tickling me. Was it a stray hair on my neck? I batted at
it.

"Ow." Oops.

"Sorry."

"Remind me never to wake you up with kisses again."
Oh god, his voice was so deep in the mornings.

"Can I have a shower?" I asked, rolling over to face
him. His eyes sparkled.

"Of course. Quick though, we need to go soon."
Groaning, I got out of bed and padded to the
bathroom.

"Towel?" I called.

"Use mine. Blue one."

"Ok." I closed the door and locked it. No way was he
sneaking in.

I ran the water. It blasted out cold but then slowly
changed to warm water. My muscles relaxed as the
hot water soothed them. I washed my hair with the
apple shampoo I found in a bottle at the bottom of

the shower. I stood there for a few minutes longer just to let the water soothe me. Turning the water off, I stepped out the shower and wrapped Jake's blue towel around me.

I walked through to the bedroom. My clothes had been neatly laid out on the bed, along with a pack of pants. Had he really just run to the shop while I was in the shower? I got dressed and went out the bedroom. Jake was in the kitchen, spreading jam over some slices of toast.

"Nice shower?" He asked as he handed me a plate with toast on.

"Yes thanks. What flavour?" I asked looking at the toast.

"Raspberry."

Checking the time on the clock above the kitchen sink, we inhaled our breakfasts and made a run for the elevator. I wasn't sure about Jake, but I hated being late anywhere. Clouds covered the sky when we got outside and it was cold. Not what you'd expect in summer, was it? People were on their morning walks, some rushing to make it on time to the bus.

Barely anyone was at the theatre when we arrived. I breathed a sigh of relief. Jake chuckled next to me. We sat next to each other in the front row of seats as Tyler came in.

"Hello you two. Enjoy your day off?" Quizzed Tyler.

"Yes thanks. I took Addy to Brighton for the day."

"I loved it." I chipped in.

"It is lovely there, I went a few years ago myself." Tyler reminisced. More people start filing in and I saw he was getting ready to start. "Freddy will be in later." He announced.

A few people muttered between them.

"We only have two weeks until our opening performance. I'm so proud of how well all of you are doing so far. I'd like to work through the script scene by scene for final checks that it's all perfect. Nora needs some people for costume checks, Jake and Addison are the only two she's completely finalised with." He paused for breath. "Can everyone who's dancing in the ball go to see her please?" A lot of people got up and left. As they were just extras for the ball scenes, I didn't know any of their names. Tyler called up the actors he needed for the first couple scenes. Jake and I stayed put in our seats, our legs ever so slightly touching.

We watched Ella growing up, and we watched her grieve with her father when he mother passed away. If I hadn't have seen this scene multiple times before, I might have cried a little It was so upsetting to see a young girl lose her two parents within three years of each other. My dad walking out on us had been hard enough. Tyler had changed the story slightly so that Ella was raised by the house staff after her parents died. I wasn't a big fan of his script change, but it would do. Hopefully the audience liked it instead. Soon enough it was time for some of the scenes with me in. We worked through each scene with ease, having already rehearsed over a million times. Well, it felt like a million. With every movement I made, I was beginning to feel my stage fright slowly slipping away. *I could do this.* I was going to perform as Cinderella in two weeks' time and I wouldn't freak out or get sick. My confidence in myself was beginning to lift. I'd come so far since my GCSE days.

When the extra people had come back, we ran

through the ballroom scene. Oh how good it felt
having Jake holding me. I'd longed for it all day, but
we hadn't snuck a moment together. He had a hold
on my waist with one hand and held my hand up with
the other. We waltzed around the centre of the stage.
It felt as though it was only the two of us there,
dancing our way to happiness.

The set for every scene was complete and perfect. It
fit every scene exactly, the ballroom pieces were
gorgeous. Tyler had opted to use the fountain I'd
painted for the castle garden as well as in the wedding
scene.

The run through went well, Tyler was really proud of
it.

"End of the week we'll do a costume run through."
He said to us.

I couldn't wait to put on my wedding dress again, I'd
felt so good in it. Jake had complimented how good it
looked on me and I couldn't wait for him to look at
me that way again. Next week couldn't possibly come
fast enough.

All of the step sister's dresses had been fitted again
and were now ready. I'd had so much fun today, I
couldn't wait to go home and tell mum all about it. I'd
kept her updated on where I was the last two days I
hadn't been home. She was buzzing about how I'd
been with Jake all weekend, she'd be like an excited
puppy when I told her the details over dinner that
night.

We were finished before the evening after two run-
throughs. Freddy didn't turn up in the end, I
wondered if he was alright. It was dusk when we left.
I meandered down each dark street on my way home,
figuring out what story to feed my mum. I'd leave out

the events from after the club visit. I reached my street and she pounced on me as soon as I unlocked the front door.

"Tell me everything!" She squealed, hugging me. Sometimes my mum wasn't the adult she was supposed to be.

"Ok ok. Let's cook dinner and then I'll tell you." I laughed.

We made ourselves burger and chips. Mum had been trying to eat our way through the freezer for months. We made ourselves comfortable while we ate.

"So tell me." Mum said through a mouthful of beef burger. "Did he treat you well?"

"Yes, he took me to Brighton yesterday and we had the best day." My eyes lit up as I replayed the memories of the past few days in my mind.

"How lovely, you've always wanted to go there, haven't you?"

"Yes. We went to an arcade and had a beach day and went back to his flat."

"And did you share his bed?" Oh God. Now I was doomed. I could either deny it, or she'd find out later. I had two options and I didn't know which one to take. Mum surveyed my silence. "Sweetie I just want to check you're safe and well."

"I'm fine." I whispered picking up a chip and dipping it in tomato sauce. She eyed me inquisitively.

"So did you?"

I nudged her. "Muuum. But out!" I laughed. "If I ever need advice or help I'll definitely come to you."

We made eye contact and burst into laughter. She used to push me for details about the boys I was with but I think she's slowly backing off as I grow up. She hadn't pushed me much about Jake so there was progress already.

Dress rehearsals were horrible. Some actors picked at their costumes or were too bothered about them to actually focus. It was our first dress rehearsal, and the last rehearsal before the show. I was so nervous to be going onstage. Performing in front of the cast was ok because mistakes were always made in the production process. It was a whole different story in front of an audience. My name would be in the programme beneath my picture so everyone would know my name and face. What if I messed up and everyone in the town made fun of me?

I made my way to the theatre slowly, still lost in my thoughts. I was late. Late because I hadn't set an alarm like I was supposed to; I just hoped I wouldn't be in trouble. I knew I would be the last one to arrive. I silently prayed that I wasn't desperately needed at that moment. I had the folders in my bag that I'd been given on my first day, I figured it was best to bring them back to give to Stefan, my stage assistant replacement. It really did feel like I was lifting weights at the gym. Struggling, I opened the theatre door to join everyone else. All eyes turned to me as I stepped in, making loads of noise as I managed to whack the folders against the door.

"Addison."

"I'm sorry I'm late. I did try calling." I stammered.

"Yes and I got your message. Please join us."

I waddled down to sit with everyone else. Tyler cleared his throat and Freddy continued talking from where he was before I'd interrupted.

"Dress rehearsals are the most important. It's the one where the director's vision is brought to life. It's the final check that all costumes are ok so costume designers know if any final work needs done before the big day. It's an important day. We'll be focused mostly on lighting today."

He looked at Vanessa.

"Vanessa, we need to find a sequence for the ballroom scene. It needs to be pretty and different colours so it may take a while to finalise a sequence that goes well."

"Got it, I'll start on that straight away." Vanessa said and she got up and made her way to the lighting box at the back of the hall.

"The rest of you are free unless Nora needs you and until I need you."

I stayed sat where I was. Jake rose out of his seat and sat next to me, resting a hand on my thigh.

"Are you alright?" He asked.

I rubbed my forehead. "Not really, I'm not feeling too well." I replied.

"Stay here." He got up and left.

I turned my attention to the stage, where the extra dancers were practising. They twirled around countless times. The lights changed through a sequence of different colours. There were blues, pinks, purples.

Jake returned a short while later carrying a bottle and a small box. He passed me the bottle.

"I went and got you paracetamol."

"Thanks." Gratefully I took two tablets from the strip he passed to me. I swallowed each one with a sip of water.

"Just think, it's only a week now until our first performance." He whispered.

"I know, I'm so nervous." I fretted.

"You'll be great. I know you will." He left a delicate

kiss on my temple. My body turned to jelly beneath his touch. He ran his hand through his hair, damp from a shower. My head was pounding, my vision starting to blur around the edges. I closed my eyes then opened them again. "You ok?"

I got up out my seat, thinking walking would help. I tripped coming out the row of seats; then everything went black.

CHAPTER 9

I came to and found myself in a strange room. There were cushions beneath me and a blanket over me. The room was tiny, barely any form of decoration. I could hear someone breathing nearby. I gently opened my eyes.

"Thank goodness you're alive." Vanessa was sat on the floor by my side. Her eyes were full of concern. "Drink this." She passed me a glass of water.

"Thank you." I took a few sips and felt the col liquid rush down my throat. I went to sit up and she put her hand on my back.

"Easy, you had quite a fall."

"I wasn't feeling well, what actually happened?" I asked groggily.

"Jake said you got up out your seat and tripped. Although it looks more likely that you fainted." She slowly helped me sit up. My heart palpitated for a few moments then resumed beating as normal. How long had I been out of it? I asked just that.

"About half an hour."

"Jesus."

"Yeah, but as long as you're ok."

"Where is everyone?" I rubbed my eyes.

"Final checks for everything."

"Jake?"

"Onstage probably, rehearsing and worrying about you. He freaked out when you fainted."

"I need to see him, tell him I'm ok. How did I get here? And where are we?" I asked, my mind confused and only just registering the fact that I was no longer in the main theatre.

"Jake carried you out; we're in a backstage room that never really gets used. Thought you'd want the privacy when you woke up."

"Thank you. I really appreciate that."

Vanessa helped me to my feet and we slowly made our way back to the main hall. Discreetly, I opened the door, with Vanessa's help and shuffled in. Jake jumped off the stage and launched himself into my arms. He held me in a strong, supportive grip and I snuggled my nose into his neck. He pulled back.

"I was so worried about you." He murmured looking me dead in the eyes. I felt my knees become jelly at how his eyes sparkled. He pressed a kiss on my forehead. "Are you okay?"

"Yes thanks. I'm ok. Thanks for carrying me to a quiet room; it really helped not having everyone in my face."

"No problem sweetheart." He laid a kiss on my temple.

Tyler came over to us. "How are you feeling?"

"Better."

"Good. Do you feel up to participating?"

"Can I see how I feel for a bit and try later on?" I

asked.

"Of course."

"Thank you."

The rest of the day ran smoothly. I took part in a bit of final rehearsals but had to sit down after a short while. Jake kept watching me all morning to see how I was. Tyler dismissed us for our lunch break just after midday. By then I'd had painkillers and was beginning to feel better.

"What is your plan for lunch? He's given us just over an hour." Jake asked as he stood next to me again.

"I want to go out, but I'm not too sure. I don't know where I'd like to go."

"Are you feeling well enough to go?" Concern was etched across his face.

"Well I'll need to be won't I? Otherwise how on Earth will I get myself home?" I laughed.

"Well I'd drive you home if you wanted it."

"Let's go out for lunch and see how that goes."

"Sure."

Together we walked through the polished lobby of the theatre and out onto the street. Turning right, we headed down the high street. There was a little café down that way that I loved and that was where I was leading Jake to.

It was a small little thing, not much room for tables. It had been the place I sought comfort in throughout college when I was stressed and didn't want to be cooped at home any longer then I had to be. I'd taken my old best friend there on weekends occasionally; it had slowly begun to become our main hang out space. The outside walls were painted gold, the trim painted cream. The front had two full size windows that showed off the full view outside. Granted the only thing you could see were the town hall and any pedestrians walking past.

The interior design was lovely and floral. Small tables were scattered around one side of the café. Each table had a floral patterned tablecloth on with hedgehog pattern place mats. The walls were decorated with various painting and framed photos of waterfalls and beach scenes. That was why I found it so peaceful when I was there. The counter was on the other side, tucked away in the corner with a doorway to the kitchen in the corner of it.

Jake and I sat on a table at the back of the room. Quiet. I needed quiet to keep my head straight and keep myself intact. The menu was small, but it was good. They did sausage rolls, pasties, baguettes, sandwiches and paninis. They served a small variety of hot drinks, with a fridge full of cold drinks next to the counter for you to select your own. I knew exactly what I'd be having: hot chocolate and a chicken, ham and onion panini. The staff in here knew me well, they also knew I ordered the same thing every time I was in here. Jake flicked his eyes over the menu.

"The usual Addison?" Kirsten asked.

Kirsten was the waitress who'd sat by my side while I cried during the tough times and had gotten herself into trouble for it. She was one of the kindest people I knew. She had black hair streaked with grey and her bright blue eyes had started to darken over the last couple of years. Stress and pain didn't ever bring that woman down and I admired her so much for her strong spirit. She had a bubbly personality and would always try her best to bring a smile to the faces of everyone who ate in the café.

I lifted my eyes to look at her. "Of course. What else

would I have?" I laughed.

"You're right hun, you never change. You do you."
She noted my order down on her little order notepad
before turning to Jake. I kicked his ankle from
beneath the table. He clicked out of the reverie he'd
been trapped in.

"I'd like the Meaty Baguette please and a latte."

"Anything else at all?" Kirsten asked us.

"No thank you."

Kirsten turned on her heel and carried our order to
the kitchen. Shortly after we heard the sound of her
frothing milk on the wan of the coffee machine. She
filled the group head with coffee grounds and turned
on the machine. I watched as she filled two espresso
cups before pouring one into the bottom of a latte
glass. She poured the milk into the glass and scooped
out the froth with a teaspoon and placed it on top. To
make my hot chocolate she mixed milk and hot
chocolate powder together before heating it up using
the wand again. She poured the chocolatey hot milk
into a big cappuccino cup, put both on saucers and
carried them over.

I smiled gratefully and the smell of chocolate.

"Mmm, thank you." I said, inhaling the smell from
the wafting steam.

"You're welcome. Your food will be ready soon."

"You come here a lot?" Jake asked as he raised an
eyebrow and took a sip of his latte. I always let my
hot chocolate cool down slightly before I drank it so I
wouldn't burn my tongue.

"I used to all the time through college. This place was
where I'd come to relieve my stress. Kirsten, our
waitress, was always the one who'd sit and listen or
help me find solutions to what had gone wrong." I

explained, gesturing to the walls around us.

"I'm glad you had a place to escape to."

Moments of silence passed before Kirsten brought us out our food. My eyes widened at the sight of food and my stomach growled in agreement.

"Thanks Kirsten" I called to her already retreating figure.

Jake had obviously been desperate for food too because he'd already started eating into his baguette. I picked up my knife and cut diagonally into my panini. *Mmm.* I took a bite and moaned at the different tastes on my tongue.

"Did you just have a foodgasm?" Jake asked, laughing.

"Maybe. You have sauce on you face." I pointed out.

"That's fine, I'll get it off once I'm finished."

Without responding, I carried on eating. Our time was running out so I began eating a little bit faster. I finished before Jake did so I went to get a couple of napkins so he could wipe his face when he was finished. Passing him the napkins, I sat back down. I sipped at my drink while I waited for him. He wiped his face with the napkins before gulping down the rest of his latte. I finished my hot chocolate then I went to find Kirsten to pay.

After I'd paid, with Jake protesting the whole time, we made our way back to work, hand in hand. He had his fingers laced through mine. Electricity pulsed through my veins, my heart filling with lust. Slowly strolling back to the theatre, I watched all the wildlife around us. I watched the trees dancing in the wind and butterflies flapping about around us. Bees pollinated every flower, their floral scent filling the air. Wind stroked every petal of each flower, every leaf on each tree. Dogs barked at each other as people walked them too closely to one another.

We got back to work in just enough time to spare. Most people had already come back if they hadn't stayed.

"One final rehearsal and then it'll be show time." Freddy announced. "From the top please."

So we ran through our final rehearsal.

CHAPTER 10

Opening night.

Tonight was our first performance of Cinderella. Holy crap was I nervous. I was shaking when I woke up that morning. My anxiety was at its peak already, heaven help me before I went onstage. Mum had booked herself a seat to watch so I felt more pressure on my shoulders to make her proud. I showered and dried my hair before plaiting it and going down for breakfast. Well, considering it was more midday, it was more like lunch at this point.

"Good luck for tonight darling." Mum said as she looked up from the soup she was stirring on the stove top. That would be what we'd reheat when we got home tonight. I was too full of nerves to eat anything now.

"Thanks mum. Is that for when we get back tonight?" I asked, gesturing to the soup.

"It will be. What are you having for lunch?"

"I'm not hungry." I told her.

"You need something. You missed breakfast and you

won't have any dinner until late tonight so you're
having something."

Sometimes my mum was so stubborn. I was happy I
hadn't received that gene from her.

"I'm too nervous mum and if I eat I'll be sick. I don't
want to relive what happened last time I went
onstage. Remember how I was sick last time?"

"You won't be sick honey. You're going to be my
brave girl and you're going to ace this performance
tonight."

"Mum, did you really say I'll 'ace' it?" I laughed.

"Yes, isn't that what you kids say these days?"

"Yes but no."

"How can it be both?"

"Because it's weird when parents say it."

"Alright then." We stood in silence for few moments
before mum spoke up. "Oi you cheeky mare, you
forgot to tell me what you want for lunch." She
scolded as she nudged my ribs playfully.

"Something small if you're forcing me to have
something."

"My tomato pasta?"

"Too filling."

"A bowl of curly fries?" Now that was something I
could never turn down.

"Yes please."

Mum walked over to the freezer while I turned the
dial on the oven to preheat. It took a while to heat up
before we could put my fries in.

"Go watch a film or something, it'll take your mind
off it a bit."

"Ok mum." I kissed her cheek briefly and went
through to the living room. I turned on Netflix and
was half an hour in when she brings out my curly

fries. "Thank you." She passed me the bottle of ketchup. I drizzled some across the top of the bowl of chips. Mum came and sat on the sofa beside me whilst I ate.

"You'll need to leave soon sweetie so you aren't late."

I checked my phone.

"Shoot, is that really the time?"

"Yeah."

"I'll see you later then mum. I love you." I said as I ran to get my shoes on.

"Good luck!" Mum called as I left the house. I ran to the bus to make it on time.

"Addison!" Freddy exclaimed as I arrived to the theatre. "You alright? You look really nervous."

"Oh I am." I watched as his face spread into a grin.

"You'll do great, have some confidence in yourself."

"That's exactly what I *don't* have." I told him.

"You will."

We spent the afternoon double checking the lighting and moving the scenery to the correct angles and markers for the opening scenes. The further through the day we got, the more anxious I became. I tried taking deep breath, but they weren't really doing very much. I tried thinking of other things, not the show, but it didn't help when everyone kept asking if I was ready for the show. I wanted to scream at everyone to go away but thought against it. All I needed was some peace to get to grips with my emotions.

Before I knew it, evening came and people were starting to arrive. I heard echoes of chatter and commotion from behind the curtain. I was stood on the side of the stage in my first costume, ready to go on for my first scene. Creeping across the stage, I took a peek at how many people were in the audience.

We were almost full of people. I felt sweat beading my forehead. Freddy came over after half an hour. "Showtime people!"

This was it.

The day, the moment I'd been dreading.

Our opening performance.

I had to go up in front of loads of people and try to keep it together. I felt a panic attack rising up my throat. The curtains were raised and the performance began. They watched Ella growing up and I heard a few sobs when her father died. Her step sisters kicked her out her own room and that was that.

"Ella, your room is the biggest so give it up for your sisters." Lady Tremaine demanded.

I looked up at her from my place on the floor, soot covered my face from the fire.

"So what room will I move to? Am I swapping rooms with them?" I asked her as I stood up.

"You'll have the attic."

I looked at her with upset and confusion. "Oh. But there is no bed up there?"

"Take your mattress up with you. Get it done by midday tomorrow."

Over the course of the "day", I moved all my belongings to the attic. Anastasia was kind enough to help me. Then it was the ball. Ella, Cinderella as they'd renamed her, was left behind until her fairy godmother appeared. She performed her spell and then I twirled around and around until my ragged dress turned into my gorgeous ball gown.

It was a gorgeous baby blue silk with thin shoulder straps and a balloon skirt. Butterflies were embroidered in its bodice. I had on white silk shoes.

I arrived at the ball and found myself in the company

of the prince. I felt so honoured to meet him outside the ballroom.

"Would you like a dance?" He asked, bowing and extending his hand out to me. I took it and he placed one hand on my waist. We waltzed through to the ballroom and joined the other dancers. I danced with Prince Charming until the spell had begun to wear off.

Panicking, I said "I have to go. Goodbye!"

"But why? Where are you going?" Prince Charming called as he ran out the ballroom with me.

The rest of the performance ran without a hitch. My anxiety and stage fright faded the longer I was up on the stage. Jake found me after the show had finished and scooped me into a hug.

"You were brilliant!" He said as he picked me up and spun me around.

"Thanks."

"We're doing more shows together, me and my girl." He smiled and leant down to press his lips to mine. I parted my lips and he deepened our kiss. My hand wrapped round his neck and he gripped onto my waist tighter.

That was how we started a career in theatre together. He'd built up my confidence since I'd met him and he'd helped me to push through so much.

HOW DO YOU LOVE SOMEONE

CHAPTER 11

Two years ago

Jake's lips met mine as the curtain fell. Cheers erupted
from the audience, but in that moment, it was just us,
lost in our kiss, our thoughts consumed by each
other.

"You were perfect," he whispered. I could only nod in
response, too stunned to speak. I had done it. I had
starred in a performance on stage, something I'd
always been too afraid to attempt in life. I felt proud
of myself, and I could see the pride in Jake's eyes.

"It was still terrifying!" I laughed. "But I'm so glad I
did it. Thanks for believing in me."

"Of course." Jake wrapped his arms around me,
holding me close.

"Well done, everyone," Freddy announced as we
exited the stage. Makeup had been stashed away
during the performance, and dressing rooms tidied.
Nora had neatly folded my everyday clothes on a

bench, alongside the other girls' garments. The female actors entered the dressing room, and we changed in silence, the rustling of clothes the only sound. No one uttered a word.

My thoughts turned to my mum, waiting for me as soon as I got dressed. I had spotted her in the third row, wearing the biggest smile I'd ever seen. Happiness radiated from her in waves.

I handed my wedding dress back to Nora, who smiled appreciatively. "Thanks, love. Well done today."

"Thanks, Nora. I can't believe how incredible it felt to be up there, in front of everyone."

"I can't wait to see what else you accomplish in your new acting career. I'll be keeping an eye out for your name on theatre billboards," Nora chuckled.

"I wouldn't go that far."

"Why not? You're talented, Addison. Don't turn your back on it," she replied as she walked over to hang up Cinderella's wedding dress.

I returned to the theatre to find my mum but froze when I saw her in the back corner, engrossed in conversation with a man she seemed to have bumped into. I watched as she threw her head back in laughter, and he responded with a warm smile. I hadn't seen my mum laugh like that in years. I left her to enjoy her conversation and headed backstage to find Jake.

I searched through various rooms, but it wasn't until I heard a voice behind me that I found him.

"I'm right here, baby."

I spun around, greeted by Casual Jake instead of Prince Charming Jake. He wore his usual jeans and black shirt, holding a small bouquet of roses.

"These are for you because you made me so proud tonight," he said, offering me the roses. I accepted them with gratitude, inhaling their scent.

"They're gorgeous, Jake. You didn't need to get me flowers just to show you're proud of me."

"Well, what else could I have done?" he asked.

I grinned. "Well, we could do an encore of two nights ago."

"Cheeky girl!" He chuckled softly, pulling me into his arms. "But seriously, you were amazing. I couldn't be more excited to see how far you'll go in this career, with me."

The words "with me" were all I needed to hear to keep pursuing theatre. I had been content to leave that show as a one-off, returning to my role as backstage crew.

A man in a suit approached us. "You're the stars?" he asked me, his deep, wealthy-sounding voice resonating.

"Yes," I replied hesitantly.

He extended a business card. "I'm searching for talent that can excel in this industry, and you, darling, stood out tonight. I sense you lack confidence in yourself, but I can help you improve that. Give me a call anytime, and we'll keep you informed about shows that might interest you."

"Wow, thank you." My jaw dropped at his praise.

"I look forward to hearing from you, Addison. I'm Mr. Reynolds."

"It's a pleasure to meet you," I said, extending my hand. He shook it before walking away in the direction he'd come from.

"Oh wow," Jake said, just as stunned as I was. "See, baby? I told you that you were talented."

Nora and Jake had been right; I was talented, and other people recognised it. I was determined to climb higher in this career, with Jake and Mum by my side.

CHAPTER 12

Present Day

Sunlight crept through the window, stretching its long fingers towards the foot of the bed. I rolled over and smiled at the sound of soft snores next to me. Jake and I had moved in together a little over a year ago after our second theatre production together. Both of us had applied to audition for multiple productions, and rarely had we failed to secure a part in the ones we took part in. My onstage confidence had begun to blossom as time had passed, and I'd starred in more shows. Jake had gotten a role in a performance of Matilda, and he was a bit sceptical about the musical aspect of the show. He could act, but after having heard him in the shower, I severely doubted his singing skills. That was a performance I needed to see him in!

I yawned and moved closer to him as his snores became fewer and farther between. He'd wake up soon. Almost as soon as I'd gotten comfortable against him, Jake woke up.

'Morning baby,' he murmured, still half-asleep.

'Morning,' I replied as I leant up to kiss his cheek. He opened an eye, and I grinned. Jake stroked my cheek lightly before leaning in to kiss me. His soft lips brushed gently against mine, and I sucked in a breath. Every kiss we'd shared had always made me feel just a little more in love with him; they were full of love. Finding the flat we lived in had been a journey and a half. We'd visited many places, put deposits down on some only to have them refunded when someone offered the full amount in cash. I'd wanted to give up at that point, but Jake had been full of optimism, so we continued looking. A few months down the line, a flat in the city centre had become available, and we'd snapped it up.

Admittedly, we'd struggled in the beginning with the flood of things needed to furnish the place the way we'd imagined it. It had taken a while for me to get used to the routine change from what I was used to. The day I'd moved out had brought tears to my eyes. My childhood had been packed into little more than ten boxes, marking the start of a new chapter in my life. I'd been upset about leaving Mum behind, but she'd moved in with my soon-to-be stepdad. Knowing that she would be looked after had made leaving home a little bit more bearable. I was excited to be moving in with Jake; we'd been together for two years now, and it just felt like the right decision for both of us. We were together almost every day when we worked on the same stage shows, and we lived much closer to the theatre than I had before. It was only a few roads away now, compared to the bus journey I used to take every day when I was a part of Cinderella.

'Time to get up,' I declared. I giggled as Jake hit me with his pillow.

'Please, just a few minutes longer,' he begged, giving me his puppy dog eyes.

'Nope, because we said that yesterday, and we spent all day together in bed. Not happening, we're going out,' I announced as I pulled the duvet back and touched my toes to the soft navy-coloured carpet.

'Out where?' he groaned at my enthusiasm.

'Uh, I haven't actually decided yet,' I hesitated. 'But I'll think of something. Come on, lazy bones!'

'Addy, I love you, but sometimes I wish you weren't so energetic in the mornings,' he moaned as he ran his fingers through his dishevelled hair.

'I love you too,' I grinned. Jake stuck his tongue out at me.

By the time I'd devoured breakfast to feed my ravenous stomach, Jake was up and ready to go out. He was simply in a shirt and shorts, the same clothes he often wore.

'Are you alright?' he whispered as he kissed the back of my head.

I yawned. 'Yes thanks. Grab something to eat, and then we're going on a walk.'

'Before ten in the morning? Seriously, Addison?'

'Yes.'

He groaned in response and fried himself an egg while I set some things to record on our TV ready to watch tonight.

The sky was a beautiful shade of blue, with a gentle breeze blowing through the trees. Leaves danced on their branches. We walked slowly through the town and walked past Jake's old flat building.

'It all started here,' I sighed.

'No love, it started in the theatre,' Jake replied, smiling at the memory.

'We met there, yes, but I didn't fully fall in love with you until that first night I stayed round.'

'Ah yes, that night. Fancy a remake when we're home?' he winked.

I shoved him playfully. 'Definitely not!' I laughed. I started jogging and screamed as Jake raced behind me to catch me. He chased me down the road until we reached a green space with people walking dogs and children playing.

'Okay okay, you win,' I panted, completely out of breath.

'Yes!' Jake punched the air in victory.

'You won't... always win,' I panted. He rested a hand on my back while I caught my breath again. 'Let's go, I'm okay.' Jake took my hand in his and laced his fingers through mine before we continued walking.

It was rare that the two of us had days off together. Even if we were part of the same production, sometimes I was needed for scenes on days Jake wasn't. Careers in theatre didn't give much time for leisure. Today was a day of pure bliss together. Young love, as my mum would say. Between productions, we'd spend our days together, whether on walks or cozied up in our flat, enjoying each other's company. But with Jake now working on a show and me still auditioning, there were some days I'd wake up alone and times I'd fall asleep alone because he stayed late. I never complained; I knew how important his career was to him because mine had always been important to me. I wanted to build a life together with Jake, and that meant time apart sometimes. We dreamed of having a house rather than a flat and our children running around, watching us on stage and being proud of their parents. I wanted a family, and I prayed Jake wanted one eventually too.

Children played in the park, and older ones played football on the green. I gripped Jake's hand tighter, and his gentle squeeze caused heat to flood my veins. Jake stopped walking and lay down between a couple of trees at the edge of the green.

'Lie with me,' he said.

'Why?' I asked, hiding my amusement.

'It's a gorgeous morning, and I want to enjoy it with you.'

I smiled and gently laid myself down beside him. Noticing the gap between us, Jake shuffled closer towards me and snaked his arm beneath me to hold me to him. I rested my head just below his shoulder, and he lightly stroked down my arm.

'I love mornings like this. Peaceful and blissful,' I stated, playing with a piece of grass between my fingers. The morning air was crisp and fresh.

'It's a perfect way to spend the morning,' Jake agreed. I twisted my body to look at him, and his eyes were sparkling in the sunlight.

After a few moments, he spoke again. 'Addy, I challenge you to see who can find the most peculiar shaped clouds.'

'And what is the prize?' I asked. I never competed unless the winner got something.

'Loser buys lunch for the two of us, wherever, whatever the winner requests.'

'You're on,' I laughed.

What felt like hours passed with the two of us laughing over shapes we saw in the clouds.

'Alien!' I shouted. 'I win!'

'You cheat!' Jake laughed, playfully poking my ribs.
'No, the last one you saw was what you thought was a
chicken. It was a dog,' I cried as he tickled me. I
flipped myself so I was pinning him to the grass. 'See?
I win.' I laughed.

Jake reached up and stroked my cheek before cupping
my face and pulling me to him. His lips brushed mine
gently, and I parted my lips. Then it sunk in.

'Oi, now who's cheating? Jake, you can't win by
giving me kisses in the hope I surrender the victory of
beating you again.'

'What if I wasn't trying to win, and I just wanted to
kiss my girl?' he asked, his voice low and husky. There
was a playful spark in his eyes. I rolled my eyes and
pressed a soft kiss to his lips before jumping up.

'Come on, loser, I'm hungry.'

Jake laughed and followed suit. Hand in hand, we
walked around the perimeter a couple of times before
changing direction to the high street. It was almost
midday, and the sun was at its peak in the sky.

'Where are we eating?' The loser asked. I was still
grinning with my victory.

'I don't actually know,' I trailed off. There weren't
overly many places to eat where we lived; we were a
small town, not a city. Without a word, I led him
down a side street towards my favourite little café.

Jake sighed. 'How did I guess we'd end up here
again?' He laughed.

'Maybe because you know it's my favourite?'

'Mm, there is that I suppose.'

It was a tiny café with a pink and white awning, the
outside walls a pastel blue colour. A small silver bell
above the door tinkled as we entered. The strong
aroma of cake and coffee wafted up my nose, and I

smiled. It was a small café, tucked away from the
bustle of the main street. Tables and chairs were
scattered around the room, with plaid tablecloths
hanging off each table, almost in piles on the floor.
An older couple occupied a table in a far corner,
holding hands and smiling deeply into each other's
eyes. They didn't flinch at the sound of the bell.
I discovered Tina's Tea Shop about a year ago when
my other favourite café closed due to the owner
moving to France. Tina's did cake and hot drinks,
with the most delicious hot chocolate I'd ever had.
'Corner,' Jake said, pulling me towards the corner
table by the front window. He liked to sit where he
could watch people as they walked past.
'Okay.' The cosy interior created a happy atmosphere
that warmed hearts on rainy days. We tucked
ourselves in at the table, and, as always, Jake picked
up the menu. I always chose the same thing, as he
often did too, but he liked to see the menu 'in case
they add something new,' he'd tell me.
'I don't need to ask what you're having,' Jake said as
he scraped his chair back and went to the counter.
I let my thoughts wander away and let my mind flood
with previous memories. I struggled to remember the
days before Jake let light flood my heart and helped
me face my demons. He'd been by my side through
shows, my mum's new marriage, and now here we
were, going into our twenties together.
Mum had fallen in love with a man she'd met at my
very first performance, the one where I met Jake. In
the weeks that had followed, they'd gone out almost
every night and were married two months ago. They'd
gone on their honeymoon to Spain and had left me
their keys to look after their cat. It had felt strange

being in my childhood home without Mum around to pester me about the early days of my relationship with Jake.

'We'll be gone for two weeks,' Mum had said, hugging me and kissing my cheek before taking Sam's hand to their waiting taxi. 'Lily only needs feeding two times a day; she's a house cat, so don't worry about her being out all night.' She informed me as she passed me the front door keys.

'I'll miss you,' I said, hugging her tighter.

Mum laughed. 'Don't be daft, you have Jake for company.'

'Yeah, but I'm stuck with him every day.'

'I'll call you, sweetie, don't worry.'

'Don't worry, Addison, I'll look after her!' He called.

'I know you will!' I called back, smiling. I hugged them both for the last time before watching them drive away to the London airport.

Snapping back to reality, I caught sight of Jake coming back with a tray in his hands.

'Everything okay, baby?' he asked as he laid it gently on the table between us.

'Yeah, I was just thinking about how lucky I am to have you and how happy Mum is since her wedding.'

'Yes, they do seem quite in love, don't they?'

I nodded. 'I might go and visit them tomorrow; would you like to join me?'

'I don't see why not.' He shrugged. I smiled. After I'd devoured the biggest slice of chocolate cake I could ever dream of, we began walking back home. Jake had offered to get me something hot to eat, but the cake had filled me up. Holding the door open, Jake rested his hand on the small of my back and guided me out of Tina's.

The sky had become grey, with clouds that looked like they'd drown out our happiness. The streets were full of people shopping; it was difficult to navigate our way through. We laughed and joked as we walked, drawing a lot of attention to ourselves, but we didn't care. We were happy, and I wanted everyone to know it. We laughed the rest of the way home until we reached the end of our street.

Fumbling around in my pockets, I looked at Jake. 'Do you have your keys?' I asked him. The flat door didn't let you in unless you have a key.

'I thought you had yours?' he asked, confused.

'No, I thought you picked it up.'

'Great, so we've locked ourselves out,' Jake sighed, throwing his hands in the air with frustration.

'Seems like it.' I laughed. 'I guess I was too excited to come out that I didn't think about it.'

Jake became silent for a few moments as he processed what I'd said. 'Didn't we give your mum a spare key?'

'Yes! Yes, we did. I'm sure she'll come and let us in.' I pulled my phone out of my pocket to dial her number before Jake took it from me. 'Hey!'

'We'll go and see her; you haven't visited for a while.' That was true; I hadn't seen her since she'd gotten home from her honeymoon. I was overdue for a visit.

CHAPTER 13

The sun shone down as we walked away from the town centre towards my mum's house. Sam had made a few changes since he'd moved in, but not many, starting with the garden. Where it had all been weeds growing up, it was now full of brightly coloured flowers ready for summer, and I smiled to myself as I watched butterflies and bees flying from flower to flower. The gravel path to the front door had been tidied compared to the zigzag it used to be. The front door had been painted white to stand out against the red bricks that made up my mum's house.

'Let's hope Julie and Sam are in,' Jake said, slipping his fingers out of my grip so he could knock on the door. Mum had never owned a doorbell; she couldn't stand them. Jake knocked the door firmly before stepping backward. We heard keys jingling in the hallway and something fall on the floor.

'Oh, bugger,' I heard Mum moan, 'I'll be there in a moment!' she called.

'It's ok, Mum, it's only me.'

Mum opened the door, her hair messy and clad in her dressing gown.

'Addison? What a lovely surprise, come in.' I stepped through the door, and Jake followed closely behind. 'How are you both?'

'We're alright, thank you,' Jake nodded. 'Your daughter has a favour to ask.' I couldn't believe he'd blamed me! He'd been the last one out of the flat door that morning.

'Oh dear, Addy, what have you done now?' Mum asked, concern etching across her features.

'Not much, except Jake locked us out and neither of us have a key to get back in,' I admitted. Ha! Take that, Jake.

'Me?' Jake laughed.

'Yes, you.'

I followed Mum into the living room. It was still the pale-yellow walls and leather sofas I'd grown up with; I was glad nothing had changed since Sam had moved in. Potted plants lined the shelf above the fireplace with a couple of photos of me as a child.

Memories of my early teenage years flooded back to me. Mum and I would dance around this room with Katy Perry playing loudly. Our neighbours got annoyed, but we didn't care; it wasn't something we did often. I remembered having sleepovers with my friends when Mum was working late, and I was home by myself.

'So how did you manage to lock yourselves out? It's not like you to not take a key,' Mum asked as she picked up her mug from the coffee table.

'I was desperate to get Jake out for a walk, and I thought he'd picked up his keys because neither of us normally leaves without them.' I took Jake's hand affectionately in mine.

'Yes, well, she hasn't told you the part where she was going to call you rather than actually come and visit,' Jake dobbed me in.

'I didn't know if you were home!' I defended. I turned to face Jake. 'What if she'd been out? It would've been a waste of time walking her to find she wasn't home.'

'I guess so,' he sulked. He hated it when I had a point against him. One point to me.

'Oh dear, you two,' Mum laughed softly. 'We were hoping you'd let us borrow your key so we could get back in.'

'Stay for dinner, and I'll drive you both home,' Mum offered. 'Or did you have plans?'

Jake looked at me, and I shook my head. 'We'd love to stay, thanks, Julie.'

'No worries. It's pasta for dinner.'

'Perfect,' Jake said.

'Excellent,' I agreed. Mum's pasta had always been my favourite meal growing up. 'Where's Sam?'

'He's often at work late, sweetie. You might get to see him before you go home.'

'Cool.'

'Jake, how is your new musical going?' Mum asked. Tuning out the conversation, I went into the back garden. The patio was mossy, and the metal bench slightly rusty. Sam hadn't got around to sprucing up the back garden. I sat on the bench and looked around me.

Sometimes I missed the days when I lived with Mum. We always had enjoyable evenings, and we got to spend every weekend together. I loved living with

Jake, I really did, but we didn't get days off together. I know that happened when you start working, but I wished it didn't have to happen to us. Most evenings Jake got in, ate dinner, showered, and went straight to bed. I never had roles that required me to stay late, so I spent afternoons at home, alone. I had been beginning to wonder whether a pet would keep me company when Jake was out, but I wasn't sure if he'd approve of the idea.

We'd talked about having a family in the future, but never about owning a pet. We'd spoken about the life we wanted together and what he wanted to achieve with me by his side. After that was when we'd moved in together, and I'd discovered he wasn't the usual guy. Most men lived messily, but Jake cleaned up every speck of dust he could uncover, and it drove me nuts. He tidied away things that didn't need moving, and he'd often hide them in a place that I could never find.

Sunlight flooded the garden as the sun emerged from behind a cloud. I basked in the sunlight as it warmed my body. I jumped as something brushed against my leg. Looking down, I saw Mum's tabby cat.

'Hello,' I said as the cat began to purr loudly. She meowed and jumped on my knee. 'Ow,' I yelped at the feeling of her claws digging into the flesh on my thighs. She looked up at me, and her bright green eyes bore into my hazel ones. I stroked her under her chin, and her purrs became even louder. Her purrs echoed.

'What are you doing out here?' Mum asked, making me jump.

'Just thinking,' I replied.

'About?'

I debated with myself over whether to tell her about how I was feeling. 'Nothing, don't worry.'

'Ok, if you're sure.' I nodded at her before following her back inside the house. The strong aroma of pasta wafted through the hallway leading to the kitchen.

'This smell brings back so many memories,' Mum reflected as I felt Jake wrap his arms around me.

'It does,' I agreed. Turning to Jake, I asked, 'What were you two talking about when I was outside?'

'Nosey much,' he admonished.

'Yep.'

'We were talking about your childhood,' Mum admitted, stirring the steaming pan of pasta.

'Oh dear,' I put my head in my hands.

Jake and I left shortly after dinner, keen to be home for the evening. The afternoon had flown by. As a trio, we'd watched the sunset together before Mum passed us our spare flat key, and we began walking home.

'It was nice seeing Julie, wasn't it? Shame Sam wasn't there too.'

'Yeah, I think Mum misses me as much as I miss her. Hardly anything's changed at home since I moved in with you.'

The evening air was cold and bitter on my face. Spring wasn't supposed to be cold; it was a warm season. Jake's favourite season. We weaved down alleys and main roads to get home. He gripped my hand tightly when we noticed a group of large men coming towards us down an alley a few roads from home.

They were a lot bigger and more muscular than Jake was; they'd beat him if they started a fight. As they grew closer, I noticed one was staggering while another held onto him.

'You're beau'iful,' one guy slurred.

Jake straightened up. 'Yeah, she's also mine.' He snapped.

The drunken man turned his eyes to me; they were glazed and bloodshot from the alcohol. I wrinkled my nose at the smell. He had a rather full bottle of beer in his free hand.

'Sorry, mate,' the guy holding him said. 'He's a bit off it at the moment.'

'It's ok, just keep him away from her,' Jake growled. The drunk man stumbled towards me, and I hid behind Jake. 'You're ok, baby,' Jake whispered. 'Just keep walking.' He swapped hands and held me in his left hand, keeping me close to the wall. The alley was dark, there were no streetlights except for where the alley met the main road. I crept slowly along the wall, Jake covering me the whole way. He glared at the men as we passed. The sober one smiled apologetically as the other yelled drunkenly.

Once we were past, I quickened my pace to get us as far from them as possible. I didn't slow my pace until we were out of the alley.

'You can slow down, Addy, you're ok,' Jake said, beginning to sound out of breath.

'Are you sure?' I asked, stopping dead in my tracks. I looked around me and saw the brightly lit high street, our flat in the distance. Jake stopped by my side and looked deeply into my eyes. Taking a deep breath, he pulled me gently into him and pressed a delicate kiss on my forehead.

'Let's get you out of the cold,' Jake said.

CHAPTER 14

A chill pervaded the flat upon our return. I shivered. "I'm going for a shower to warm myself up," I informed Jake as I untied my shoes. A glint appeared in his eyes.

"Wait for me," he said, kicking off his trainers.

"Alone," I asserted. He halted, puzzled.

"Are you alright?"

"Yes, I'm fine," I snapped, storming down to the bathroom.

"Addison!" he called after me.

I slammed the bathroom door shut and locked it, then took a few deep breaths. Stripping, I stepped into the shower, letting the hot water relax my muscles. Music played softly from my phone as the water cascaded down my body. I allowed my mind to wander until I heard my name.

"Addy, there's a letter here for you. It looks important."

"I'll be there in a minute," I called out. After rinsing the soap from my body, I stepped out of the shower, wrapped a towel around my naked form, and found Jake in our bedroom.

"Here you go," I took the envelope from him and felt a rush of shock as I read it.

"I'm invited to audition for a Broadway musical!" I squealed.

"Really?"

"Yes!" I jumped up and down, still clutching the letter.

"Babe! That's amazing! Even better if it's down here, that'll attract loads of people," Jake exclaimed, hugging me tightly. I laughed at the sight of his wet shoulder when I pulled back.

"It's in London," I murmured. "They'll pay for my accommodation for the time I'm up there."

"What? For how long?" Jake asked, his face growing serious.

"The whole summer."

"Oh."

"I won't accept if you'd rather I stay," I said, putting the letter down on the table beside me.

"No, you should go. It's an amazing opportunity for your career. We'll make the most of our time together before you go," he smiled.

"Starting with tonight before we sleep," Jake added with a suggestive grin.

"Jake!" I exclaimed with laughter as he picked me up and carried me into our bedroom. He closed the door before throwing me onto the bed.

"What are you doing?" I asked.

"I told you. I'm making the most of our time together. Starting now," he whispered, kissing my neck gently.

"What if I stay?" I gasped as he tickled me.

"Then I'll still make the most of every moment we spend together."

His lips crashed onto mine, and I laced my fingers into his hair, pulling his face closer to mine. I felt his hot lips against my neck as he kissed down my throat. His hand dropped to my hip, keeping me still beneath him. He pressed himself against me, and my body jolted from the shock of it.

"Ready?" he asked breathlessly. I arched my body up to him to show my response. I reached up and slipped his shirt above his head, stroking his warm chest with my fingertips.

"I'll never tire of this," I sighed happily.

"Tire of what?" he asked, tucking a strand of hair behind my ear.

"Us."

"Good."

His lips returned to mine with the most delicate of kisses.

"I love you," I gasped as his fingers trailed along my thigh before resting on my hip again.

"I love you too," he moaned as I pulled his hair gently. Our lips remained locked on each other before I pulled away.

"We need to sleep," I said against his lips.

"Please," he begged.

I kissed his nose gently. "Alright."

Sunlight crept through the curtains the next morning. I opened my eyes slowly and felt a warmth spread through me as Jake tightened his grip on me in his sleep. This was how I wanted to wake up each day. Would I manage four months alone in London? Did I want to go? Would it be the right thing for me to do in this moment?

I had never liked to be away from home, let alone alone for the whole summer in an unfamiliar city. Although this was the biggest career opportunity I'd been given so far, my thoughts were all over the place on whether to take it. I'd be away from my family and friends, unable to visit home due to being so busy with rehearsals.

I needed to clear my head.

Carefully, so as not to wake Jake up, I slipped out of bed and took some clothes into the bathroom. I got myself dressed, left a note on the kitchen counter for Jake, and left the flat, locking the door behind me.

A gentle breeze made the branches sway. Couples walking dogs strolled down the street as I crossed towards the park. I needed somewhere peaceful to think. Seagulls flew overhead, squawking at each other over bits of food on the ground. I quickened my pace; I'd always been afraid of birds.

I sat on a bench by the pond in the park and watched the swans as they glided atop the water's surface. Butterflies flew around me, and birds chirped in the trees above.

This was a huge opportunity for me, for my career. I could be in a Broadway musical and be discovered by many other people and hopefully work in more shows. Jake and I would move to various places and possibly tour the country. Was that what I wanted for myself? Did I want to be a big name, or did I want to stay as I am?

Jake was happy here; he wouldn't move and leave everything behind. People made sacrifices in love, didn't they? Did I sacrifice this opportunity to stay with Jake? We'd gone through so much for me to throw it all away. So many thoughts buzzed around in my mind. No, that was my phone buzzing.

"Hello?" I answered.

"Addy, where have you gone? I got your note. Are you okay?" Jake asked, concern thick in his tone.

"I'm just trying to clear my head," I replied, tucking my hair over my shoulder and out of the wind. "I'm in the park."

"I'll be down in a minute."

"No, Jake..." I said before the call ended. My eyes welled up with tears.

A football landed at my feet. I looked up and saw two boys running toward me.

Picking up the ball, I asked, "Is this yours?"

"Yes. Please can we have it back?" one of the boys asked. They looked like twins, no more than eight years old. One had ginger hair, the other blond. Their bright blue eyes sparkled in the sunlight. I held out the ball to the blond twin.

"Here you go."

"Thank you," he smiled as he took the ball from me. He turned to go back to where they had been playing.

"You're really pretty," his brother said to me.

I blushed slightly. "Thank you," I replied, shyly.

"Troy! Anthony!" their mother called from across the park.

"Coming!"

Both boys smiled before running back to their mother, kicking the ball between them as they went. I prayed it wouldn't land in the pond.

I returned my gaze to the sky. Clouds drifted in front of the sun, casting a shadow over the ground.

"Addy!" I was pulled out of my reverie at the sound of my name. Jake was jogging toward me, his hair mussed from the wind. It was slightly damp, suggesting he'd gone for a quick shower before coming out, or he'd already had one before he'd called. "Are you okay?"

"I think so," I smiled, patting the space next to me. Jake sat down and wrapped an arm around my shoulders.

"What's wrong?" he asked.

"The letter. I can't help wondering if I shouldn't go," I admitted, playing with a blade of grass and ripping it in half.

"Why wouldn't you want to go? This is an amazing opportunity you've been given!"

"I don't want to leave you behind," I sighed. "Or Mum."

"Julie, Sam, and I will be fine," he smiled, pulling my hair away from my face. "This is about you; don't worry about any of us, okay? We'll all still be here when you're back from London."

"Four months? What if..." I trailed off.

"What if what, baby?"

"What if you find someone else when I'm gone?" I asked, looking away as tears pooled in my eyes.

"Trust me, I won't. I'll call you every night as soon as you're out of rehearsals. We'll still have time together, just far apart."

"I guess so," I muttered.

"I'm proud of you for getting the letter, of course I am, but if you choose to turn it down, I understand. Although I personally think you should accept it."

"Why? You want me to go away?" I asked, shocked at the idea.

He sighed and ran his fingers through his hair.

"You've been invited to audition. You've not been promised a part, so auditioning for the part isn't bad because it's not promised you'll earn the role."

"I guess trying isn't that bad, and if I don't get it, then I can come home, right?"

"Of course, and I'll be in the flat waiting for you."
"You wouldn't pick me up at the airport?" I gasped mockingly.
"Well, yeah, obviously I would. I'll drop you off too if you go."
I nuzzled my head into his neck and processed everything he'd just said. We sat there for a few moments, watching the swans as they swam gracefully.
"So? What are you thinking?" he asked.
"I suppose there's no harm in trying out, is there?" I asked.
"No, there isn't," Jake smiled.
"Then I guess I'm going to London."
I couldn't get over the fact that I'd agreed to go to London. I knew that auditions didn't guarantee a part in the musical, but I was giving myself the possibility of being a part of Broadway. What was wrong with me?
I was the type of girl who didn't like to leave her house much, let alone her town for what could become four months or longer.
I felt like I had just made the worst decision of my life. I'd agreed to leave my home behind just to be in a musical when everything that kept me happy was right here. I was so stupid. Why had I agreed with Jake that this was a promising idea? I was due to leave in a matter of days for the audition. We'd sent an email accepting their offer, knowing a letter wouldn't arrive in time, and Jake had begun looking at travel costs and which hotels were better. The whole time, I felt numb as he talked about how great this was for us. I just nodded along with what he said.

"We have a week until you leave, a week to go on as many dates as I can cram in and give you enough love to last a lifetime," he said, closing the lid on his laptop after paying for my hotel. Hotel costs were paid for during the production period, not during auditions. "I'll book your coach tomorrow morning."

It was midday the day after I'd agreed to go to London to audition. While Jake was up and ready to enjoy the day, I was still wrapped up in bed, hiding from everything. He'd brought me breakfast in bed, but I knew from his expression that he wanted me to get up. I wanted to do everything but that.

I wanted to revel in the familiarity of our bed, our room, our flat. If I got the part, how long would I be gone for? I wanted to stay in our flat until the moment I had to leave.

"I'm going out for a bit. Are you getting up?" Jake asked as he poked his head through the bedroom door.

"No," I mumbled.

"Are you okay?"

"I'm fine."

Jake nodded and left the doorway; I heard the flat door lock a few minutes later. I was alone. I fumbled around on the bed until I found the TV remote and switched it onto Netflix. That was how I spent my afternoon; watching chick flicks on Netflix until Jake came back in the late hours of the evening. I hadn't had dinner in case he wanted to eat together, but I wasn't overly hungry.

His hair was all over the place, and his eyes looked slightly glazed over. I leaped out of bed.

"Jake, where have you been?"

"Out with the guys," he said, stumbling through the bedroom door, slurring slightly. I ducked under his shoulder so I could catch him.

"Have you been drinking?" I asked.

"A few. I thought it would clear my head." Clear his head?

"What's wrong?"

"I miss you," he said simply.

"I'm right here," I said as I led him toward our bed.

"You won't be soon. I'll miss you. Stay."

I sighed. Stay? He was the one who insisted I go and already booked my hotel for the audition weekend.

"You told me to go, Jake. It'll only be for the summer anyway. We said we'll make it work."

"I'll come up and see you."

"Will you?" I asked, unsure if it was the alcohol talking or not.

"Yes. We'll have fun."

"Not while you're like this. Go to sleep," I said, pulling the blanket across for him to climb in.

"Ok. Come cuddle?"

Admittedly, I was a little tired. "Alright."

After covering him with the blanket, I turned the bedroom light off and went to settle into bed. Jake cuddled up against me as soon as I laid down, his arm across my stomach. I felt his hot breath against my chest, his head against my neck.

"You're so gorgeous," he yawned. I hid my smile and kissed his head. I'd always been insecure about my body, so I went silent at every compliment he gave me. He kissed my chest before nuzzling his head back against me.

"Goodnight, Jake," I whispered against the softness of his hair. He turned into a big baby every time we settled in for bed. I'd definitely miss this feeling every night.

"Goodnight, baby girl. I love you," he mumbled, his voice drowsy with sleep, as he tightened his grip around me.

"I love you too."

Jake sighed, and I was sure he was asleep. I lay on my back, wide awake, for what felt like hours. I listened to Jake's soft snores, hoping they'd relax me to sleep. Something shook me a couple of hours later. "Addy?"

"No," I told it. I was running from something; something was chasing me through the woods. Something scary that I couldn't see.

"Addison," it said again.

"Go away," I cried, the rocking motion of my body feeling like wind carrying me. My eyes snapped open after Jake poked my ribs.

"Addy?" Jake asked, his face close to mine in the darkness of our room. "What was it? Did you have a nightmare?"

I nodded. He pulled me close, stroking my hair and whispering sweet nothings against my ear.

"You're okay."

"I am now."

CHAPTER 5

Dawn broke brightly the next morning. My head rested against Jake's shoulder. I was leaving for London in six days.

'Morning,' I said as I looked up at Jake.

'Morning, princess.' Jake shifted so he was lying on his side, facing me. He leant forward, and I parted my lips slightly as he pressed his against mine. I felt all the tension and worry about London fade away as all I could think about was Jake's lips on mine. He was my own personal slice of heaven.

His arms slipped around my waist, and I became instantly aware that I hadn't taken my bra off from yesterday. I may have stayed in bed all day, but I'd put that on the second I'd woken up. His hand crept beneath my shirt, and goosebumps erupted across my skin. He flattened his palm on my back and pulled me closer. I opened my mouth for a breath, and he slipped his tongue in, teasing mine with his. I was so intoxicated by his smell, his touch, the taste of his lips on mine. I rested my hand on his cheek. We came up for breath after a few moments, and I yanked the blanket off Jake, exposing his body to the coolness of the room.

'Oi!' He groaned. I laughed.

'Up you get.'

'Says she who didn't leave our bed yesterday except for food or a drink.'

'I actually got up to pee too, unless you want me to wet the bed?'

'No thanks. It's too early. Come back here.' He smiled, lying his head on his arm and flashing me a flirty wink.

'Not a chance. You said you want to make the most of this week, don't you?'

'Yes, of course, I do.' He agreed, beginning to dry up with a pink tea towel.

'So you can choose what we do today, love. I don't mind,' I said.

'If you're sure.'

'Of course I'm sure.'

An hour later, we stood in front of the ice rink. Deep down, I was beginning to regret letting him choose what we did. His hair was messy and windblown, his eyes bright. His black coat was getting too small; it hugged him tightly around his waist.

Taking my hand, Jake smiled and led me towards the door. He paid our fees and collected our skates while I gazed over at the ice.

The last time I'd been ice skating, I'd embarrassed myself severely in front of all my friends. I'd held onto the sides and used a penguin walker and wished a hole would open up to swallow me as they all laughed at my stupidity. They mimicked everything I did until I eventually left the rink, my eyes full of tears and noticed nobody followed me to see if I was okay. That was the day I swore to myself I'd never go ice skating again so I wouldn't embarrass myself in front of anyone else. That was five years ago.

Jake noticed my hesitation when he stepped onto the ice without me. 'I won't let you fall.'

I shifted my gaze from the floor to his eyes. His face radiated optimism, and I felt myself being pulled in. 'Promise?'

'Addy, what's wrong?' He asked, worry etched across his face.

I told him my ice-skating story.

'I promise I won't laugh at you. I'll hold onto you the whole time, and I won't let you fall.'

I took his hand and followed him out onto the ice. My feet began to slide in separate directions as soon as I stepped onto the ice. Jake's arm clamped around my waist, and he helped me regain my balance. I placed my hands on his shoulders and looked up at him.

His lips pressed to my forehead. I felt a wave of heat flood my body.

'We're in the way,' Jake whispered as he acknowledged a father and two children about to step onto the ice.

We made it to the edge, with Jake basically carrying me over there. I held onto the side so tightly that my knuckles began to turn white. Jake rubbed my back reassuringly.

'You're doing great.'

'No, I'm not. I can't even stand.' I murmured.

'You haven't done this in years. I used to skate all the time growing up, so I have years of practice behind me.'

'Show-off.' I groaned as I attempted to find my feet again.

Jake took one of my hands and gripped around my waist with the other. 'I promised I wouldn't let you fall.'

He pulled us away from the edge slightly, far enough away that it was only just out of my reach. He took one step at a time, slowly to keep me balanced.

I looked around us at all the children skating around with ease. How long had they been able to skate without holding onto something? Teenagers spun around in circles in the middle of the ice. I must have looked so inadequate to them. I was in my twenties, and I had to hold onto my boyfriend for help.

I was surprised nobody was laughing at me by now. I felt like a fool.

'You're doing great,' Jake whispered, his breath hot on my ear. I blushed a little at his compliment and held onto the hand he had around me. I tried not to focus on him pulling me away from the edge.

The coolness of the ice raised goosebumps on my skin. I was glad I'd worn my jumper; it was colder than I'd expected it to be. The lights above reflected off the surface of the ice, making it sparkle.

I eventually gained the balance and confidence to skate in the middle of the rink; still holding onto Jake, of course. He fulfilled his promise of never once letting me fall. He never let go of my hand either. We skated in circles around the edge before he started to pull me further away and into the middle.

That evening, we chose to spend the evening watching Netflix with a big bowl of popcorn between us on the sofa. Jake ate most of the popcorn, though he wouldn't admit to it.

'Are you going to let me do what I wanted to earlier?' Jake asked. I saw how desperate he was for me, how much he wanted to be close to me.

Smiling, I climbed onto his lap, facing him. Jake parted his lips, and I pressed my own against them. His tongue stroked my top lip, asking me to open for him. He cupped my face in his hands, his breath becoming my own. His hand dropped to my thigh, and he began caressing it as our kiss intensified. I reached my hand up under his shirt, and he groaned at my fingers stroking up his chest.

He broke off our kiss, his forehead resting against mine. 'Go to our room.'

'No, here.' I sighed. I could feel how much he wanted me.

'Are you sure?'

'Yes.' I whispered and pressed my lips to his again. I felt a fire ignite inside me, spurring me on. Jake slipped a hand beneath my shirt and tugged it off. We laughed when I got stuck inside.

'You forgot the buttons.' I laughed.

'Shit.' He grinned, pulling it down and undoing the buttons beneath my neck. I unzipped the fly on his jeans. With me in just my bra, I lifted my body and sank down onto him. I hissed at the slight amount of pain. The hunger in Jake's eyes was unmistakable as he looked at me.

Passion filled the moments that followed. A mix of pain and pleasure ripped through my body, burned me from the inside out.

He left soft butterfly kisses in a trail down my neck, both hands holding my waist to keep me in place. I gasped at the wetness of his lips and the intensity of his touch. We were a gasping, panting mess. My body burned for him.

'I love you,' I gasped into his mouth as he kissed me again. My fingers ran through his hair, tugging the ends slightly.

'I love you too, baby,' He moaned as I sucked his neck gently, making sure to leave a mark. I lifted myself up and gently sat back down. His hands traced my curves, my thighs.

I was done for when he looked into my eyes again before we were both finished for the night.

CHAPTER 16

"This is it. My baby's off to London," Jake said as he hugged me tightly. I couldn't believe how fast the week leading up to me leaving had gone by. We'd crammed in as much time together as was humanly possible, with visits to my Mum and Sam. Jake and I had spent evenings out and late nights cuddled up. Looking at the coach to London, I knew I was going to miss being at home all the time. My hotel was paid for by Jake, and he'd given me money for food for the weekend. His eyes were watery, but he was beaming down at me. Was he happy or sad I was going away for the weekend?

"I'll miss you," he said, pressing a gentle kiss to my forehead.

"I'll be back on Monday to pack up some things if I get the part. I'm one of four people they want for this part, so I don't imagine it'll take too long for them to decide who they want," I promised.

"At least it's a show you've always wanted to see."
"Yeah, I never thought there would ever be a remote
possibility of me being asked to star in Wicked!" I
squealed, beginning to bounce up and down and
drawing lots of unwanted attention to us.
"I think you're a bit excited now," he laughed. I'd miss
that sound; his laugh. It was a deep sound, full of
heart.
"My coach leaves any minute," I acknowledged.
"I know."
Stepping onto my tiptoes, I leaned up and brushed
my lips against Jake's. His lips parted for me. He
gripped my waist, holding me in place. I wasn't one
for public displays of affection, but I couldn't help
myself in that moment. I knew I was only going for
three days at the minimum, but I'd still miss him. I'd
wake up in bed in the morning alone.
The coach driver called people to the coach. This was
it.
"I'll see you on Monday. I love you, Jake," I
whispered as I kissed his nose.
"I love you too, Addison. I'll be here Monday night
waiting for you."
I gave the coach driver my suitcase, mostly empty
with only a few clothes. I was only going to pack a
bag, but Jake insisted on buying me a suitcase in case
I bought any souvenirs to bring home for him. He
was more excited about this than I was.
I was a bundle of anxiety as the coach began to
reverse out of the station. Jake was still stood where
we'd been waiting, right in my eyeline. I smiled but
couldn't ignore the look of sadness in his eyes. He
didn't like to be away from me because of how much

time we spent together. I suppose time apart strengthens relationships, right?

As I watched Jake blur into the distance, I put my ear pods in and pressed play on my playlist on my phone. Taylor Swift filled my ears. I relaxed my body a bit and laid back on the seat; no going back now.

We drove through a few towns before merging onto the motorway.

"Alright love?" An older man asked as he sat next to me. Oh God.

The man had salt and pepper-coloured hair which was receding. He had a few teeth missing; the rest were stained with coffee. His shirt was stained, and he didn't smell like he'd showered. Please don't sit here the whole way to London, I silently prayed.

Discreetly, I turned my music up a little louder and tuned him out.

Cars whizzed past us as we drove down the motorway. I gazed out the window and watched as we passed fields full of horses and cows. My emotions were all over the place; would I succeed, or will I fail at my audition? Jake had reminded me I was only auditioning for a chance to receive the part. The closer we got to London, I could not help but wonder what he'd say if I didn't get the part. Yes, I know he said he'd be proud of me just for trying, but would he be disappointed deep down?

Morning became noon, and I grew hungry. My stomach growled, and I tensed my body, hoping it wouldn't be too loud and attract attention. Most people had headphones on or were on phone calls, so hopefully I wouldn't be noticed, except for the man next to me who kept giving me funny looks.

I almost jumped with joy when the coach driver
announced a forty-five-minute break in the journey
for people to get food. I imagined he was hungry too
after how long we'd been driving so far. We were
about halfway through the journey at this point.
The coach came off the motorway into a small service
area. After he'd parked up, the driver announced,
"Everyone please be back here by half-past one."
I got off the coach and looked around. There was a
Costa drive-through, a McDonald's, and a KFC at the
other side of the car park. I wandered towards KFC,
then changed my mind halfway and chose
McDonald's. I fancied beef rather than chicken.
It was a rather big building for a service area. Very
few cars were parked up outside, so I imagined it was
only the staff. A group of people I recognized from
the coach sped past me and through the doors. I
followed suit.
I ordered a cheeseburger and fries and took a seat
while I waited for my food.
The walls inside had paraphernalia of the company's
history. I sat reading the posters while I waited and
became surprisingly interested in the history. I hadn't
known that the first McDonald's opened as a
barbecue restaurant in 1940, or that they rebranded to
a hamburger and milkshake restaurant in 1948. I
wasn't one who enjoyed history, but I was surprised
by what I read.
"Number thirty?" A voice called. I snapped out of my
reverie and collected my food.
"Any sauces or anything?" The girl asked as I took my
food from her.
"Ketchup please," I smiled. I thanked her and sat in a
corner to eat.

I had several messages from Jake asking if I was okay. I quickly typed out a response and then began eating my food. Anxiety filled my body in a wave as I realized how close it was becoming to the audition. I was never nervous at an audition. This was a whole new feeling for me.

My phone began to buzz in my pocket with an incoming call.

"Hey Mum, are you alright?" I asked, cradling my phone between my head and shoulder as I carried my rubbish to the bin.

"Yes, I'm okay thanks. I just wanted to ask how your journey to London is going? Are you there yet?"

"Not yet the driver stopped for a lunch break. I'm popping into Costa for a drink before going back to wait on the coach."

"That's alright then. Have you been watching cars go past like you always used to?"

Every car journey we went on when I was younger, we'd always watch cars speed past us and see who could count more red cars than the other.

"Yes, but I packed a book to read so I think I'll read the rest of the way up there."

I walked out of the restaurant's door and walked across to Costa to pick up a milky hot chocolate. A chill crept over me as the sun became blanketed by clouds.

"That's not too bad then," Mum said. "Be safe up there, alright honey?"

"Yes Mum. As I said to Jake, I'll be back on Monday regardless of if I got the part or not. If I get it, I'll be back to pack, and if I don't, then it won't matter."

I ordered my hot chocolate and paid for it while Mum continued talking.

"Yes, it will matter; you've always wanted to see
Wicked with me, but I couldn't ever get us there, and
I'm sorry," I heard her sniff on the other end of the
line.

"Mum, it's okay, honestly. I wouldn't change anything
that we got up to. So what if we didn't see a show? So
what if I don't get this part?"

Mum went silent.

"You still there?"

"Yes, sweetie, I'm here."

"Are you okay?" I asked her.

"Yes."

The man at the counter called my order out, and I
accepted it from him gratefully. I nudged the café
door open and went back to the coach. Other people
were coming back.

"Are you about to get back on your coach?" Mum
asked a few moments later.

"Yes."

"I'll let you go then, please call me when you're in
your hotel so I know that you're safe."

"I will. Love you."

"Love you more."

I hung up the call and found my seat again. I began to
pull my book out of my backpack I'd packed for the
journey. I bristled as I felt someone sit next to me.

"Hello," I was surprised to hear a woman's voice. "Is
this seat taken?"

She had blonde hair that fell to her shoulders in
ringlets, heavy makeup, and she was wearing a floral
print dress.

I looked up and saw the man coming back on the
coach. No way was I sitting with him again.

"No, please take it," I said in a rush as his eyes searched for me. I shivered.

"Thank you," she said gratefully as she sat down. A strong smell of Chanel wafted up my nose. I held in a sneeze because of how strong it was. It was a strong floral smell. How much perfume did this woman use? I smiled at her before opening the first few pages of my book.

"Twilight?" She asked, looking at the cover of my book.

"Yes. I've not read it; I got it last Christmas as a present. Have you read them?"

"Yes, and they're amazing. I read them as a teenager and I still have my set, albeit battered and all. I'm Heather by the way."

"Addison," I smiled.

"That's a beautiful name."

I blushed. "Thank you."

Heather turned her attention to a message on her phone, so I turned back to my book. I used to read the days away when I was younger; I had all the free time in the world.

The remainder of the journey passed slowly. I peeked out the window several times and we didn't look any closer to London than we had been the last time I'd looked. I rested my book on my lap and closed my eyes.

"Addison?" Someone was shaking me. I swatted at them.

"Go away."

"No, unless you want to be left on the coach alone?" Heather asked.

I opened an eye.

"Don't glare at me, missy. You've basically slept the second half of the journey." She cracked a smile.

I rubbed my eyes and picked up my book. "Thank you for waking me."

"No worries, where are you staying?"

"Premier."

"I'll walk with you."

"Thanks."

Heather and I collected our suitcases and began walking to our hotel.

Anxiety flooded my body when we wove through a giant crowd. I felt my breaths get short; my chest constricted. My palms began to sweat, causing me to lose my grip on my suitcase handle. My pace slowed and Heather turned to face me.

"Are you okay?" She asked.

"Too… many… people," I panted. Why oh why did I have to have a panic attack in the street? Why had I agreed to come to London in the first place?

I wanted to go home. I wanted to be with Jake, where all my comforts were. I missed him.

Taking my hand, Heather dragged me into an alley empty enough for me to catch my breath. I leaned against the wall with my head in my hands. We stayed there for a few moments before Heather spoke again.

"Feeling any better?" She asked, placing her hand on my shoulder.

The alley she'd pulled us into was between two restaurants, an alley you wouldn't think to be empty. It was early evening, so many people were on their way out to dinner; I could hear the chatter of excitement carried through the wind.

"A bit," I managed, choking down a lungful of polluted air.

"Do you think you can go on? I won't leave your side."

"I can try," I squeaked.

We picked up our luggage again and continued our walk. I tried to divert my focus away from the swarm of people coming our way. I sucked in a breath and quickened my pace. The sooner I was through the crowd, the better.

Heather kept stealing looks at me as we walked to check I was all right; I could see her from the corner of my eye.

"It's just down this hallway," the hotel guide explained as he led me to my room about an hour later.

"Thank you, although you could have just given me directions," I replied, laughing softly.

"Now why would I do that when I could take my time to guide you instead of cleaning reception?"

My guide wasn't much older than me, possibly the same age as me. Like most people my age, he was trying to get out of doing the work he was supposed to do. He was in his posh hotel uniform, gold and purple to match the hotel's theme. His brown hair was cut short, his green eyes stood out against his tan-coloured skin. His black shoes reflected the light from the ceiling, causing them to shine. He obviously polished them regularly.

"I used to be the same, uh..."

"James," he finished for me.

"James," I repeated. "Thank you."

"Only doing my job."

"Sure you are," I said as I looked him in the eye, and we both laughed.

The hotel was very polished and tidy, not a speck of dust to be found. No cobwebs in any corners. The carpets we walked on were bright and bold, standing out against the cream-coloured walls.

James led me down all the twists and turns of the halls until we reached my room.

"303. Here we are." James handed me a key. It was heavy and golden. I took it carefully from him and unlocked the door. "If you need me, I'll be in reception."

"Thank you, James. I may need recommendations on places to eat soon if you don't mind."

"No worries."

James left, and I slowly opened the door to my room for the weekend.

I had a king-sized bed in a white-walled room. An en suite was entered straight to the left of the door to the hallway. The shower was big enough for three people with bottles of mini shower gel lined up along the counter behind the toilet. A huge ornate mirror hung above the sink.

In the main bedroom, a kettle lay on a desk in the corner of the room. Hot chocolate and coffee sachets were in a pot beside it. A plush cream carpet covered the floorboards beneath. It creaked if I walked too close to the window. The bed bounced as I threw myself on it.

My stomach growled.

I needed to find something to eat.

After James had given multiple recommendations, I chose a restaurant a couple of streets away. I sat at the bar, sipping slowly from a gin and tonic. I didn't often drink, but I thought it would help me to relax. I needed to control my feelings.

I sat alone in a corner in the restaurant. Most people threw me pitying glances. Heather was in a different hotel to me so I couldn't have invited her to join me. Slightly tipsy from one too many gins, I paid my food bill and stumbled my way outside onto the streets. I swayed my way out of the door and tripped as I stepped onto the curb.

"Easy," a man's voice said. I felt a pair of strong, muscular arms wrap themselves around my waist. Not again.

I looked up into a pair of gorgeous blue eyes. My lips parted. "Sorry."

"It's okay. Are you all right?" He asked, arms still in a strong grip around me.

"I think so," I mumbled, falling again as he stood me upright.

"I don't think you are," he laughed. "Is there somewhere I can take you?"

"Premier please."

He took my hand and led me back towards my hotel. Stars shone down from the darkness of the night sky, enveloping us in a silver glow.

"So what is a beautiful girl like you doing out this late?" His voice was deep, soothing. He had red hair, a kind smile, and gorgeous eyes.

"I'm here this weekend for an audition, and I needed to be here for the weekend," I explained as we walked.

"That's cool, what are you auditioning for? A lot of productions are coming to the Grand Theatre soon."

"Wicked. I've wanted to see it since I was a little girl," I told him, hearing my voice filling with excitement.

"That's awesome. I'll have to book a ticket."

I laughed. "We've only just met."

"And?"

"And what if I don't get a part?"

"Then I'll go anyway and pretend the most beautiful girl there is you."

My head dizzy, it took me a few moments to work out what he'd said. Had he just suggested I was beautiful? I stole a glance at his lips, wondering how he'd taste to me.

No.

Jake.

Jake was the only man I needed.

The only man I loved.

I needed to get away from this man, whoever he was. Now.

"Are you walking me all the way back?" I asked as I began to stumble along a little faster.

"Yes, and I'll tuck you into bed too."

Something flickered inside me at his words. Oh no.

"Just to the hotel will do, thanks."

"Are you sure?"

"I'm sure." I smiled.

James rushed to my side when we got to the foyer.

"Addison?"

"She's fine," Mystery Guy said gruffly.

"I'm sorry, who are you?" James asked as he looked up at him.

"Christian. I found her leaving the restaurant a bit too tipsy and thought I'd help her back."

"Fifty shades of grey?" I asked, wondering if he'd get my reference.

"No." He groaned. "Come on you, let's get you upstairs." I pushed Christian away and went towards the stairs.

I tripped, and the world went black.

CHAPTER 17

I stirred from sleep, battling a pounding headache and a feeling that could only be described as 'utter rubbish.' My eyes closed, sinking into the embrace of my soft mattress. Beside me, something shifted.

"Are you awake?" Christian's voice roused me. I shot up, my head protesting the sudden movement.

"Why are you in my bed?" My voice came out sharp.

"I wanted to make sure you were alright. You blacked out last night, and James reluctantly let me carry you up here. He just forgot to tell me to leave, so I thought I'd stay," Christian explained, inching closer.

"Did we...?" I let the question trail off.

"No, we just slept."

"Are you sure?" I asked, rubbing my eyes.

"Yes, but I wouldn't have declined if you'd asked."

I pushed him aside and dashed into the bathroom. After emptying my stomach's contents, I couldn't help but wonder what Jake was up to right now. He wouldn't have gotten drunk and ended up with another woman. Why did I black out? Why did I let myself have more than one gin? It wasn't like me.

I locked the bathroom door when I heard Christian call my name. His dishevelled appearance from sleep had made him look attractive, but I firmly told myself, 'No, Addison.'

I turned on the cold shower, hoping it would clear my foggy mind. Goosebumps erupted on my skin as I stepped beneath the cool cascade.

Today was the day of my audition. I needed to get past Christian, get ready, and make my escape.

The door handle turned.

"I'm trying to shower!" I called out.

"I need to pee and shower."

Yes! A chance to escape. I turned off the shower, wrapped myself in a towel, and unlocked the door. "All yours."

Christian's jaw dropped.

I smiled, then dressed, slung my bag over my shoulder, and left a note saying I'd gone exploring. I couldn't remember if I'd told him about my audition, but it didn't matter. I didn't need to see him again. Christian had only been a kind stranger who'd helped me back to my hotel last night.

A smile graced my lips as I stepped into the sunlight. A gentle breeze played with my hair as I aimed to navigate my way to the theatre. It wasn't too far, I recalled from my conversation with Jake. My phone buzzed, and Jake's name illuminated the screen.

"Hey, my baby girl, just wanted to wish you good luck for your audition today," he said.

"Thank you, I'm on my way there now."

"Are you nervous?" he asked, his voice filled with concern.

"Extremely."

"You'll be fine. If you get the part, I'll bring all your things up and stay with you for a couple of days."

"Really? You'd do that?"

"Of course I would."

"Thank you," I said, smiling, though he couldn't see it. I heard someone call Jake's name in the background.

"Baby, I've got to go, but we'll talk later, yeah?"

"Of course."

"Tell me how it goes."

"Jake, I won't know if I've got the part today."

"I know, but I still want to know."

I laughed. "Alright. You'd better get going. I love you."

"I love you too." Jake hung up as I arrived at the Grand Theatre.

'Grand' was an apt descriptor. It stood proudly at the end of a street, announcing its presence to all who passed by. Posters on the walls advertised upcoming performances. My grin stretched from ear to ear when I saw the Wicked poster. This was my chance.

Inside, it resembled our theatre back home. A massive crystal chandelier hung from the lobby ceiling, accentuating the opulent interior. Everything seemed to be made of quartz and crystal. The reception desk was quartz, with glass separating the ticket booth from the lobby.

"Are you here for auditions?" the receptionist asked. I snapped out of my thoughts and nodded.

"Yes, please."

She had a cheerful face, always happy. She wore casual attire; clearly, a uniform wasn't required for rehearsal days.

She led me down a long hallway to a door labelled
'dressing room.' I heard voices from the hallway.
"How many more?" a man asked, sounding tired.
"Just a few," replied a squeaky female voice.
"Alright, it's too early for this."
"Serves him right for getting drunk last night,"
laughed the woman next to me, displaying a dimple
on her right cheek. She nudged me. "Go in."
"I don't know," I hesitated. "He sounds annoyed."
"It's only because he's hungover. He's not usually like
this," she encouraged.
I took a deep breath and pushed open the dressing
room door.
"Hello," I mumbled.
"You must be Addison," the man said. I nodded,
studying his gray hair and olive skin. He had gray eyes
and wore a suit, making me feel self-conscious in my
jeans and top.
The woman beside him was blonde and youthful, her
jade green eyes contrasting with her pale complexion.
I noticed her long acrylic nails, bright and bold in
color. I shook hands with them both and sat in the
chair he gestured to.
The room felt too large to be a dressing room. It
resembled our rehearsal space back home, with gold
rails along one wall next to plush sofas.
"So, Addison, we're delighted you agreed to travel
here today. Are you tired?" the woman asked, smiling.
"A little, but nothing major."
"Okay, nervous?"
I swallowed, tucking my legs behind each other.
"No."
"It's okay if you are. Big musicals like this are a lot of
pressure," she reassured.

"Yes, I figured they would be."

She explained the performance and my role, then asked where I felt more comfortable.

"Truthfully? I prefer to be backstage. My on-stage confidence has improved, but I'm not one to jump into a leading role," I confessed.

"Yes, we understand. Phil here used to be like you."

"Aye, I did," Phil nodded. "Addison, we sent you a letter requesting you audition for a leading role."

"Yes, I'm aware, and that's why I'm here."

"But if you're more comfortable backstage, please don't pressure yourself. Daisy can arrange for the understudy we've cast to take the leading role so you can work backstage."

I pondered for a moment. Jake had been so excited about the idea of me starring in Wicked. Would he be proud if I did backstage work instead? Would he be upset? No, he'd always been proud of me, no matter what. He'd boosted my confidence, but you can't progress in life without setbacks.

"I think I'd prefer to be backstage. I'm sorry. I'm very grateful for the opportunity, though."

Daisy and Phil exchanged smiles.

"We thought you might say that," Phil agreed.

"You did?" I asked, making eye contact with him.

"I could tell by how you had to think about it. It's okay; we'd love for you to be part of the show."

"Yes, please."

Daisy wrote something down and gave me their phone numbers.

"We'll text you all the details later on."

"Thanks."

Once outside, I reached for my phone to call Jake. Would he be disappointed?

"Oh, hello, Addison."

I snapped my head up at the voice. "Christian?"

"Yes, well done for remembering me from this morning," he chuckled, and his warmth eased my nerves.

"What are you doing here?" I asked, surprised to bump into him after sneaking away earlier.

"I'm here to check out the stage for lighting and prop design," he stated, rolling his eyes as if it were obvious. My jaw dropped slightly.

"Huh?"

"I'm working on the show too."

"You have to be kidding! Last night, you said you were going to buy a ticket."

"I know you're thinking about what I said last night," he remarked, now seemingly reading my mind.

"You were going to buy a ticket, you said?"

"Yeah, I said it to gauge your reaction, but you didn't seem too bothered about it," he frowned.

"We had just met. Why would I be excited about a stranger coming to see a show I was working on?"

Christian fell silent for a moment. "I think you're pretty," he admitted, hanging his head with a sigh.

"Thanks."

"Did I interrupt something?" Christian asked, tensing at my next words.

"I was about to call my boyfriend about my audition."

"Oh. Sorry."

"It's okay, honestly," I smiled, hoping to show I wasn't too bothered.

"Does he live up here?"

"No, we live quite far from here. I'll be heading back to move some things up while I'm working on the show," I explained, searching my phone for Jake's number.

"I should go so you can call him," Christian said, shoving his hands into his jeans. The wind tousled his hair into his eyes.

"Okay."

"Before I go, would you like to go out for dinner this weekend? We'll be working behind the scenes together a lot," he suggested.

When I didn't immediately respond, he added, "Phil called me to say I'd have help backstage."

"Oh, okay. Yeah, I suppose that would be alright if I'm not back home packing."

"Cool."

"Cool beans."

Christian laughed again. "I'll see you soon, Addison. I'll have Phil text you my number, and you can decide if you want to meet up or not."

"Thanks."

I watched as he strode through the theatre doors and left me alone on the pavement. I dialed Jake's number and listened as it rang. It rang for a while before he answered.

"Hey, baby," he said, his voice husky, as if he had just woken up.

"Did I wake you up?" I asked.

"Yes, but I miss you, so it's okay," he replied, a lazy smile evident in his tone.

"I miss you too."

"So, how was your audition? I assume that's why you're calling?"

"Yes, but please don't be mad at me," I cautioned.

"Why would I be mad, babe? I told you that if you didn't get it, I'd still be proud of you for trying."

"I decided to work backstage instead," I confessed, heading towards the fairground I had heard about last night. Crossing the road, I could hear Jake's muffled voice on the other end of the line.

"That's great! I'm proud of you!"

"Really? You're not upset that I didn't choose the starring role?"

"Of course not! And guess what, babe?" His voice filled with excitement.

"What's that?"

"I've booked myself a ticket for the first show!"

"Really?" I asked, covering my mouth in surprise.

"Yes, and the producer of my show has given me this weekend off to bring your things to you," Jake exclaimed.

"Wait, what? I thought I was coming back to pack," I said.

"I didn't think you'd be up for all that traveling, and I get to spend the weekend with my girl."

We chatted for a few more minutes before Jake had to get ready to go out.

"Call me later, okay?" he begged, his puppy-dog eyes practically audible.

"Of course, I will. I love you, Jakey."

"I love you too, Addy."

We blew kisses to each other before ending the call. He was bringing everything here for me? Was he eager to get me moved for the show? I pushed the thought away and considered how I would spend the day. So many places called to be explored, but the crowds unnerved me. Taking a deep breath, I navigated through the bustling crowd to reach my next challenge: facing my fear of crowds.

CHAPTER 18

Anxiety coursed through me as I made my way towards the London Eye. It had always been a dream of mine to see it up close, and now the opportunity was finally here. Excitement bubbled inside me as I caught a glimpse of the iconic attraction in the distance.

The sky stretched out in a calming pastel shade of blue, the sun's warmth caressing my skin. Birds soared overhead, their cheerful chirps filling the air. A gentle breeze rustled through the trees, offering respite from the summer heat. The streets were teeming with people, and I found myself navigating through the bustling crowd, trying to avoid collisions. I couldn't help but wish that Jake were with me. It would have been so much more enjoyable to have him by my side. Being alone in this sea of strangers felt oddly disconcerting. I could feel the waves of anxiety threatening to engulf me, my breath growing shallow. No, I needed to confront my fears, I told myself firmly.

I moved to the side of the pavement and gazed out across the expanse of water before me. The rhythmic motion of the river helped calm my racing heart and soothe my strained lungs. Deep breath in, deep breath out. I continued taking slow, deliberate breaths and stole a glance behind me. Most of the crowd had dispersed, probably off to grab lunch, so I summoned the courage to continue my stroll.

Joining the queue for the London Eye, I noticed that it extended quite a distance. Clearly, it was a popular attraction. We inched forward at a steady but unhurried pace. After what felt like an hour, I was nearing the front of the line.

Suddenly, a tap on my shoulder jolted me from my thoughts. I turned around to find Christian.

"Are you following me?" I blurted out, forgetting to censor myself.

Christian chuckled. "Not initially."

"What do you mean, 'not initially'?" I demanded, hands on my hips.

"I saw you struggling with the crowd, so I started walking towards you. I stopped and waited when I saw you looking out across the River Thames. Then, I decided to follow you here."

"So, you're stalking me?"

"No, not exactly. More like looking out for you, I guess."

"Oh, okay. Would you like to ride with me?"

"I'm guessing you have a fear of heights too?"

"Got it in one."

"Then yes, I'd love to."

I smiled and returned my attention to the line ahead, feeling Christian step up beside me.

Finally, it was our turn. The attendant helped us into our little compartment and secured the door. It was a snug space, with Christian and me sitting opposite each other, our knees almost touching. Christian tensed slightly at the contact, and a strange sensation flickered in my stomach.

I jumped as I felt us begin to ascend from the ground. I gazed out in awe as I watched London stretch out before us, a sprawling metropolis. Roads wound around towering buildings to converge at the city center. Pollution hung in the air, a product of countless cars and homes, casting a hazy shroud over the planet. Homeless individuals sought shelter under awnings, escaping the light drizzle that had begun.

Christian cleared his throat. "What brought you to London?" he asked, his leg brushing against mine once more.

"My boyfriend thought it would be a good idea for me to accept the audition opportunity I'd been offered," I replied, tearing my gaze away from the window.

"What led you to pursue a career in theatre?"

I had never really pondered that question before. Theatre hadn't been my childhood dream. I had studied it in college alongside art and music. My original aspiration had been to become a singer and design my own album covers. Acting had never been my forte, but it seemed like the logical third choice. After all, acting and performing often went hand in hand, and it didn't feel right to leave it out.

Back in the day, I used to write songs, but I never did anything with them. I had a few audio recordings ready to upload, but I had never mustered the confidence to do it. I was terrified of becoming someone who received hate for their online uploads. When I saw the advertisement for a backstage assistant for Cinderella after finishing college, I took it to support my mum. Backstage work meant I wouldn't be in the spotlight - at least, that hadn't been my initial intention.

"And I assume you've been in many shows since?" Christian inquired.

Had I really vocalised all of that?

"Yes, usually in leading roles, but I was too nervous to take on that responsibility this time," I explained.

Christian's eyes sparkled. "Wow."

"My life isn't all that impressive," I said, downplaying his compliment.

"It is, and I'd like you to join me for dinner tomorrow night. As friends, obviously."

"Obviously," I agreed. "Really?"

"Well, we'll both be working backstage roles, so we'll be spending a lot of time together."

"Right, okay." I stole another glance out of the window as we continued to rise.

"I suppose a work dinner wouldn't be too bad."

I could see for miles out of the window.

"Great. Shall we meet at six tomorrow?"

"Sure."

CHAPTER 19

I hadn't anticipated Christian taking me to such a lovely restaurant. After all, we were just going out as friends, and he was well aware that Jake was visiting me this weekend.

The early evening bathed London in a warm, golden glow as Friday night settled in. Jake would arrive tomorrow night, bringing the bags he'd packed for me. The city was alive with people bustling on every corner. Shades of pink and orange blended behind the clouds, creating a breath-taking sunset. The sky transformed into a canvas of merging colours, while the soft chirps of birds were carried away by the gentle breeze.

"Ladies first," Christian grinned as he held open the door to the restaurant. It was an Italian gem, tucked away from the bustling main streets of London. Inside, the décor mirrored the colours of the Italian flag with patterns of red, green, and white. Old photographs adorned the walls, capturing moments from history. Neat rows of tables and chairs filled the space, dimly lit by lanterns hanging on the walls.

"Hello, do you have a reservation?" inquired a waitress, dressed in a white shirt, black tie, black waistcoat, and matching shoes and trousers. Her hair was a vibrant shade of ginger, neatly secured in a bun atop her head.

"No, but we'd like a table for two, please," Christian requested, removing his hands from his pockets. Compared to me, he was dressed for a formal date. I wore a black shirt and jeans, while he sported the same style of shirt and trousers as our waitress.

She led us to a corner table, perhaps assuming that we were on a romantic date. A small vase with roses and a candle graced the space between our placemats.

Christian reached for the book of matches beside the candle and handed it to the waitress.

"Thank you, but we won't be needing these," he said. She nodded and left us to peruse the menu. I smiled at Christian and reached for a menu filled mainly with pasta and pizza options.

"Are you looking forward to seeing your boyfriend?" Christian asked as he scanned his own menu.

"Yes, it's only been a few days, but I do miss him," I admitted.

"I can imagine, especially after spending two years together."

"He's been a great support, especially with my stage confidence over the years. Both him and my mum are my biggest cheerleaders," I reminisced, memories of Jake and Mum attending every one of my performances flooding my mind.

"It sounds like you have a wonderful support system."

"Are you ready to order?" A young waiter appeared as if from thin air, startling me from my reverie.

Christian glanced at me, and I nodded. "Yes, we are, thank you."

The waiter turned to me. "Ladies first, then."

"I'll have a bowl of tomato pasta, please, with extra garlic bread," I requested, passing my menu to the waiter.

"Pepperoni pizza with added pepper for me, please, and barbecue sauce," Christian added with a smile.

I wrinkled my nose in response.

"I'll get that through to the kitchen for you," our waiter said.

"Thank you."

"Extra garlic bread?" Christian raised an eyebrow at me after the waiter left.

"Yes, it's my favourite, especially with pasta."

"You'll definitely keep vampires at bay," he teased. I smiled and tilted my head down slightly.

Minutes passed in silence, and I began to feel a bit uneasy about accepting this dinner invitation. It was a good idea to get to know Christian since we would be working together starting next week, and that meant spending a lot of time together.

As a waiter carefully placed our food in front of us, he asked, "Shall I get the bill?"

I nodded.

After finishing our desserts, Christian suggested, "Shall we ask for the bill?"

I nodded.

I picked up my coat and followed Christian to the bar, standing just behind him as he paid for our meal.

As we left the restaurant, darkness had fallen outside. I wondered how long we had been there.

A group of boisterous men stood at the street corner we needed to pass to get back to my hotel. I slowed my pace.

"It's alright, you're with me," Christian reassured me as he took my hand. My body tensed briefly at the contact, but I relaxed as he led me past the group. Laughter erupted from them in response to something someone had said.

Our hotel gradually came into view as we walked. We were still holding hands, and I couldn't help but blush slightly.

Dropping his hand, I challenged, "Race you back!"

"Cheater! You had a head start!" Christian called out from behind me.

James waved at us as we raced through the lobby and headed for the elevators. There was little space between us as the doors closed. I was breathless from the sprint, a fact that seemed to amuse Christian judging by the grin on his face.

"Tired?" he laughed.

"Yes," I panted. "I'm not used to running."

I received the shock of my life when I opened my hotel room door. Bags were strewn across the floor, and another suitcase sat in the corner next to mine.

"Jake!" I exclaimed, throwing myself into his arms. He pushed me away, his eyes seething with anger when they landed on Christian.

"Addison, who the hell is this?" he demanded.

"Jake, this is Christian. He's working backstage on the show with me," I explained, trying to hold Jake's hand. His fists clenched.

"Have you been on a date?" Jake growled, his gaze returning to me.

149

"What? No, Jake, that's ridiculous!" I cried, my jaw dropping at his accusation.

"Then what the hell is going on here?"

Christian cleared his throat. "I took her to dinner as colleagues to learn more about who I'd be working with on set."

"So it was a date," Jake growled. "You're a liar," he pointed at me.

"Jake?" I questioned.

"I came to surprise my girlfriend, only to find her bringing another man up to her hotel room."

"No, Jake, that's not what's happening," I tried to explain.

"I don't believe you."

"I was making sure she got back safely, man. I know she's your girl."

Jake fell silent.

"Jake?" I squeaked out as a tear slipped down my cheek.

"I'm going back home, Addison. I can't do this. Good luck with the show."

"Jake, please!" I begged.

"We'll talk later, okay?"

"Please, Jake. I love you!"

"I love you too," Jake said before picking up his backpack and leaving.

CHAPTER 20

As Jake stormed out, his footsteps echoing in the empty corridor, I grappled with the overwhelming urge to chase after him. Christian sat on my hotel bed; his eyes locked onto the bags Jake had brought with him.

Had I just irreparably damaged my relationship with Jake? He thought we'd been on a date, and that mistrust was gnawing at my heart. But deep down, I knew Jake. He understood that my love for him was unwavering, that I would never betray him. He knew me better than anyone else.

Tears streamed down my cheeks as I stood there, staring at the door through which Jake had escaped. He was gone.

"Addy?" Christian's voice was gentle as he got up and placed a comforting hand on my shoulder. I turned, unable to hold back the sobs any longer, and buried my face in his neck. I let the tears flow freely, my cries echoing through the room.

"Shh, it's okay," Christian murmured soothingly, his hand running through my hair. In the warmth of his embrace, I held onto him tightly, our bodies pressed close.

"He's gone," I wailed, the pain and uncertainty tearing at my soul.

"He'll come back," Christian reassured me, his voice unwavering with conviction. "He loves you."

"What if he doesn't anymore?" The fear clung to my words, drowning me in a sea of despair.

I turned my head to catch sight of the bags Jake had brought up for me. It felt as if my entire world had crumbled beneath my feet, leaving me in a desolate void.

But I needed to gather the shattered pieces of my resolve, to reclaim the strength that had once defined me.

What was it they said in theatre rehearsals?

"On with the show..."

FORGET ABOUT US COMING LATE
2025

SNEAK PEEK OF FORGET ABOUT US

CHAPTER 1

Rain slashed down from the sky, soaking us both. His eyes pierced mine, locking my gaze so I couldn't move. We didn't know this would be our final night together. At least, I didn't.

His fingers brushed my chin, his lips pressing ever so gently to my own. I couldn't help the grin that spread across my face. Rubbing my nose against his, once, twice, I lifted my hands to his shoulders and kissed him again. Something I didn't recognise flickered in his eyes for a moment.

The rain continued to pour, but we just stood there, wrapped in each other's arms and getting completely drenched. I didn't care. It was only water, I wasn't going to melt like the witch from The Wizard Of Oz. 'I have to go.' He whispered. I nodded. His lips pressed to mine once more, more desperate this time.

We'd known each other for years, grown more and more in love that whole time. It didn't feel like he was saying goodbye. I knew he had to go, I could see his brother waiting in the car behind him, so why was he just standing here?

'I love you.' He said, for the last time, before turning around on his heel and getting into his brother's car. I watched as they drove up and around the corner.

He didn't look back.

ABOUT THE AUTHOR

Hope has wanted to be an author since she was 13. She's loved to read for as long as she can remember and is often found either reading in her bedroom or on her laptop typing away with a new novel. She studied catering at college because of her love of baking. Her first novel, Up In Flames was released 2 months after her 18th birthday and she began writing her next book as soon as she'd sent it off.

She is always active on Instagram and Facebook.

Facebook: Hope Wilkie-Summers
Instagram: hwilkie05

Printed in Great Britain
by Amazon

56083636R00096